About the Author

Camilla is an engineer turned writer after she quit her job to follow her husband on an adventure abroad.

She's a cat lover, coffee addict, and shoe hoarder. Besides writing, she loves reading—duh!—cooking, watching bad TV, and going to the movies—popcorn, please. She's a bit of a foodie, nothing too serious. A keen traveler, Camilla knows mosquitoes play a role in the ecosystem, and she doesn't want to starve all those frog princes out there, but she could really live without them.

You can find out more about her here: www.camillaisley.com and by following her on Twitter.

@camillaisley
www.facebook.com/camillaisley

Also by Camilla Isley

Romantic Comedies

Stand Alones
I Wish for You
A Sudden Crush

First Comes Love Series
Love Connection
I Have Never
A Christmas Date
To the Stars and Back

New Adult College Romance

Just Friends Series
Let's Be Just Friends
Friend Zone
My Best Friend's Boyfriend
I Don't Want To Be Friends

MY BEST FRIEND'S BOYFRIEND

JUST FRIENDS BOOK 3

CAMILLA ISLEY

Dedication

To all best friends who are in love with the
same person…

One

Haley

Now

"I don't have an umbrella," Haley called, shouting to be heard over the rumbling summer storm. "Do you?"

"No," David yelled back. "And I don't care."

He hurried past her out of the cover of the library porch and ran down the steps. When he reached the bottom, he tilted his face up and closed his eyes. In a matter of seconds, he was soaked.

"What are you doing?"

David looked at her from across the street, he was walking backward toward the center of Harvard Yard. "Come here. It's only water."

Haley didn't know what possessed her, but she did as he asked. She ran off the porch and joined him in the middle of the park. The sensation of the rain on her skin was electrifying as she spun on her toes, arms opened wide. Haley looked upward and laughed and laughed, unable to stop—until she pirouetted right into David's arms. The smile died on her lips as he caught her wrists and held her hands close to his chest, leaning his head down…

She tried to pull back, a ragged breath catching in her throat. "David, don't."

David's lips brushed her forehead in a soft, wet kiss. "I wasn't going to," he whispered. "The next time we kiss, you'll want to just as much as I do now…"

Two

Madison

Two Months Ago

Madison fled the room and closed the door behind her, pausing a moment in the hall to catch her breath. Her hand was still wrapped around the doorknob, and her rib cage bobbed up and down in panicked gasps. Tears blurred her vision, and her temples were exploding with a mix of fear, shame, and the first signs of a killer hangover. Now that she was alone, the enormity of what she'd almost done hit her in the chest, guilt stabbing at her heart. *No*, she didn't have a second to spare thinking about the betrayal. Her number one priority was to get the hell out of her grandparents' house.

The Smithson country mansion was a two-story building with ten plus bedrooms and a three-acre garden with a pool. Even if the property belonged to her grandparents, Madison and her cousins had basically grown up here. But now the familiar walls of the upper-floor hall seemed to be pressing in on Madison, ready to crush her in their wake.

No one was up here, save for the people in the room she'd just left. Madison let go of the handle as if burnt by an electric shock and stumbled down the hall. She hopped down the stairs, careful not to trip on the hem of her bridesmaid dress, and paused on the last step to check the ground floor. The gardens were swarming with wedding guests, but the house itself was empty except for a few servers scurrying in and out of the kitchen.

All clear.

Running as fast as her high heels would allow, Madison covered the distance from the bottom of the stairs to the main door in a blur of lavender silk. Then she was out. No one had seen her, no one had called after her.

Good.

She could have handled a random relative or a guest, but if she'd run into Alice, or worse, her mom, they would have seen right through her. And what if she'd run into Georgiana?

The thought made her shiver, making her walk across the front-yard-turned-parking-lot all the more difficult. Her spiky heels kept sinking into the fine white gravel, causing her to stumble with every step as she traipsed toward her car. Madison considered taking off her shoes, but she doubted walking barefoot on pebbles would prove any more comfortable.

A few more wobbly steps got her to her SUV.

With trembling hands, she fished her car keys out of her clutch to unlock it, then collapsed into the driver's seat. Only after hauling the door shut and putting a darkened window between her and the house did Madison finally feel safe.

She rested her head back against the seat, closing her eyes and taking a few deep breaths. When she'd calmed down enough to drive, she kicked off her shoes, threw them onto the passenger seat, and put the car into drive. But the row of cars parked in front was too close for her to get out. She maneuvered the car back and forward a few times, trying to steer it at an angle that would allow her to exit, but the SUV was too big.

Losing any composure she'd just tried to recover, Madison started screaming and crying, hitting the wheel in violent blows of desperation. Why did nothing in her life ever go according to plan?

"Why? WHY?" She kept shouting it over and over again. "WHY?"

When her throat began to hurt from the screaming, and her hands started to go numb from slamming her palms against leather-covered plastic, Madison instead gripped the wheel and desperately turned her head left and right in search of a solution. But she was one hundred percent trapped. What now? She couldn't go back to the reception and seek out the cars' owners. No, there were too many people on her "avoid-at-all-cost list" she didn't want to risk bumping into: Ethan, Vicky, Rose, Alice, Tyler, Georgiana…

With a sinking heart, Madison realized she'd never be able to show her face at another family gathering ever again. Later; she'd think about all that *later*. Now she had more pressing issues to solve. On a whim, Madison glanced at the rearview mirror—behind the SUV was nothing but spotless green grass and an intricate flower bed.

Well, sorry, Grandma, Madison thought as she switched the gear to reverse.

She hit the accelerator with enough force to jump up the curb separating the lawn from the gravel and reversed into the flower bed. Pushing the gear back to drive, she pressed her foot all the way down and the car screeched forward, leaving deep tire marks in its wake. Her grandparents' otherwise pristine front garden, ruined. She'd never hear the end of it if they found out it had been her, but at the moment she was too frenzied to care. Half of the family already hated her, so why not start working on pushing away the half that still cared about her?

The drive home seemed to take forever. When Madison finally pulled up in front of her building, she was still feeling nauseous. The pounding at her temples had not stopped, and the stomach-churning anxiety gnawing at her guts had not passed. She parked the car in her reserved spot, killed the engine, grabbed her shoes and clutch, and got out of the SUV barefooted holding up the hem of her dress—without heels, the skirt was too long.

Halfway to her building, Madison stopped dead in her tracks. Jack Sullivan was sitting on the front steps with a forlorn expression—the look of someone who'd been waiting for a long time.

Perfect. Just freaking perfect!

If there was one person missing from Madison's "avoid list" at the wedding, it seemed the dude had decided to show up at her place instead. Oh, he wasn't here to see her—she knew that. Jack was here for Alice, her roommate. But the last thing Madison needed right now was to be reminded of another guy who'd used her for easy sex and then forgotten all about her. Of another time she'd been too quick to jump in bed with a dude she'd just met. Of another betrayal that had almost cost Madison one of her best friends.

Jack didn't look like he was about to go away anytime soon, and Madison was too exhausted to wait for him to leave. She needed a shower, her bed, and a Xanax. Keys clutched tightly in her hands, she marched forward.

"Madison, hey," Jack said, jumping up. "I

was—"

"Leave me alone," she replied. "I don't want to talk to you."

"Oh, okay." He backed off a step. "Do you know when Alice will be home?"

"I said leave me alone!" Madison yelled, brushing past him and shoving her key into the lock. She let herself in, then slammed the door in Jack's shocked face.

To hell with him, too.

In her room, she wrestled with the zipper to get out of the gown, threw the shoes in a corner, and headed to the bathroom for a hot shower. Thankfully, the apartment was empty. No one around to ask her what had happened or to demand an explanation for her shitty behavior, which she still didn't begin to understand herself.

Yes, her life was a mess. Guys hated her, or used her and then threw her in the garbage once they'd had their fun. And her cousin Georgiana was the queen bee of bitches. *But nothing can justify the fact that I almost slept with Georgiana's husband on their wedding day.*

Was it because she'd wanted revenge? Or was she just so pathetic that even the most insignificant flattery from a handsome man made her lose control of herself?

"What's wrong with me?" Madison asked the empty bathroom.

She tried to wash away the shame and humiliation with the scorching water, rubbing her skin raw until it was all blotched and red. But no amount of scrubbing could cleanse the emotional stains off Madison's conscience.

Wrapped in a towel, wet hair loose on her shoulders, Madison collapsed on the bed ready to forget she existed. Unfortunately, the world wasn't as ready to forget her. Just as she was starting to doze off—thanks only to anti-anxiety drops—her phone rang. The muffled ringtone came from inside the clutch she'd dropped on the desk, only a few feet away from the bed but out of reach. Madison glared at the small bag, resentful someone had woken her when all she wanted was to be unconscious. She was pondering what would bother her more—to keep listening to the ringtone, or to get up and silence it—when the sound died on its own. *Finally, something goes right for once.*

But Madison had only just started getting cozy again on the pillows when the ringtone filled the room once more. This time, she dragged herself out of bed to find out who was calling.

Vicky.

Despite the way her cousin had reacted back at their grandparents' house—preferring comprehension over judgment after walking in on her sister's husband kissing a bridesmaid—

Madison groaned. She stared at the phone still ringing in her hands, but couldn't bring herself to answer. The shame was too much. No matter if Vicky was the most understanding person in the world, Madison wasn't ready to talk to her. Filled with guilt, she let the call go unanswered, hoping her cousin would give up.

It didn't happen. Nothing ever happened the way Madison wished it to. When Vicky called again, Madison let that call, too, go unanswered. Then she turned off her phone and sank back on the bed, finally sure nothing would distract her from the void of her existence.

At some point she dozed off, and she must have slept for a few hours, because when she woke up the sun was starting to set. Madison straightened up against the headboard, her neck sore from falling asleep on wet hair. She blinked, trying to clear her vision. A shiver ran through her entire body; the air conditioning in the apartment was set on a low temperature, and the towel she'd been wearing had almost entirely slipped off.

Madison rubbed her arms with her hands, then climbed out of bed and went to fetch a pair of clean PJs. She was just pulling on the bottom half when the buzzer rang. Had that been what had woken her up?

Gingerly, she shuffled through the living room to the entrance hall. Their building had video intercoms, and their camera showed a distressed Vicky fidgeting with the button. She was still wearing her bridesmaid dress—an exact replica of the lavender gown now adorning the floor of Madison's room.

What now?

Madison didn't want to talk to her, but Vicky must've been worried sick to rush all the way here as soon as the wedding had ended. I should have texted her to say I'd gotten home fine, but didn't feel like talking, not left her hanging. Can I do anything right?

Well, there was no escape now. Vicky was here, probably wondering if Madison had died in a horrible car crash. Madison picked up the receiver just as the buzzer rang again.

"That's my buzzer you're abusing," Haley's voice drifted out of the intercom. "Can I help you?"

Madison's eyes snapped to the small screen on the wall. Haley—her other roommate—had just walked into the frame, and was now talking to Vicky. The girls seemed unaware Madison could overhear them.

"Yeah, sorry," Vicky said. "Hi. I'm Victoria Smithson, Madison's cousin. I was looking for her."

Haley gave Victoria a once-over. "Didn't you see her at the wedding?"

"Yeah. But I wanted to make sure she got

home okay."

"Couldn't you call?"

"Her phone is off," Vicky said, looking annoyed. "Is there something wrong with me wanting to see my cousin?"

"No, of course not. It's just that in the two years we've lived together, this is the first house visit any of her relatives have paid her. Odd, right? Especially since you've spent the entire day together." Haley's cold logic wasn't missing a beat. "Did something happen?"

"No!" Vicky was too quick to say, and Madison could pick up Haley's skeptical expression even on the tiny black-and-white screen. "I only wanted to check if she got home safe."

"Well, her car is in our reserved spot." Haley pointed to the side and then crossed her arms. "Doesn't seem damaged in any way, so we can assume everything's fine."

"I'm sorry, but do you have something against me?" Vicky snapped. "Why can't you just let me in?"

"It's nothing personal, but don't you think that if Madison wanted to talk to you she'd have her phone on? Or she would've let you in herself." Haley turned toward the camera with a pointed look.

Instinctively, Madison took a step back. It was

as if Haley was staring right at her through the screen.

"Listen, something did happen," Vicky said. "It's a family matter, and I can't discuss it with you, but Madison and I need to talk."

"Yeah, the problem is I can't shake the feeling Madison is doing her best to avoid you. If something is bothering her, she can talk to me."

"No!" Vicky yelled, frustrated. "She can't talk about what happened with you."

"Uh-oh, why not? Is she forbidden? She's not a kid you can boss around, you know."

Vicky stuttered something intelligible, her embarrassment bound to confirm Haley's theory.

Madison's roommate instantly went on the aggressive. "Aren't you supposed to be the good cousin?"

"I *am* the good cousin…"

Madison couldn't watch any longer. "It's okay, Haley," she said into the speaker. Both heads snapped toward the intercom. "Vicky is only trying to help."

"Oh, Madison." Vicky stepped so close to the camera that her face took over the entire screen. "Are you okay?"

"Yeah, I'm fine. Sorry I didn't pick up the phone, I was too…" She couldn't say, *"Ashamed."* "Well, you know, I didn't feel like talking."

"Madison, you need to talk to someone," Vicky insisted.

"Does it have to be you?"

Vicky turned sideways and looked at Haley. "You really stuck your neck out for my cousin."

"She's my best friend," Haley said simply.

"Please take care of her tonight, and whatever she tells you, please keep it to yourself."

"You can trust Haley," Madison jumped in. "She won't say anything."

"Seems I've been outvoted," Vicky sighed. "I'm going home, Madison. When you're ready to talk, please call me, okay?"

"I promise. And, Vicky… thank you."

Madison watched her cousin wave toward the camera as if to say she had nothing to be thanked for, and then Vicky turned on her heel and disappeared off the edge of the screen.

Haley frowned at the camera in an "explanation time" way, and said, "Since you're there, why don't you buzz me in?"

Madison took a deep breath, then pushed the button. This was not a conversation she was looking forward to.

Three

Madison

Madison positioned herself on a stool at the kitchen bar with a direct view of the entrance to wait for her roommate's arrival. The few minutes Haley took to ride up in the elevator and reach the apartment seemed to last forever. When she finally got in, Madison's heart was in her throat. Talking about the wedding fiasco would force her to admit what had happened, even to herself.

"So," Haley said instead of *"Hello."* "Who do I have to beat?"

"Me, unfortunately," Madison replied, getting up from the stool. "I'm the villain in this one."

"You?" Haley hung her jacket on the rack behind the door and dropped her backpack on the carpet. "What did you do?"

Before confessing, Madison sought the comfort of a hug, clinging to Haley and collapsing on her shoulder in a fit of sobs. Haley caressed her hair and murmured soft, soothing words.

After Madison had calmed down enough, Haley said, "Get in bed, I'm making tea."

Madison followed the order and waited under the covers for Haley. She came in a few minutes later with two steaming mugs and settled next to her, sipping the tea and waiting for when Madison would be ready to talk.

Between muffled sobs, Madison managed to spill out everything. "At the wedding, I kissed the groom," she confessed. "Georgiana's husband. Ethan and Rose walked in on us making out in one of the guest rooms. Ethan and Tyler began to fight and Rose was trying to stop Ethan from smashing Tyler's face when Vicky came into the room and took charge of everything. She gave Tyler a pep talk and tried to calm Ethan down, then she sent me home," Madison concluded, keeping her sad tale as short as she could. At the end, she turned toward Haley, prepared to find judgment and disappointment written all over her best friend's face and finding neither.

"Okay," Haley said. "Now I can see why Vicky was so worried about someone outside the family knowing."

"Because I'm a horrible person, the worst."

"You only made a mistake. Okay, a big one, but that doesn't make you a horrible person for life. What I don't understand is…" Haley frowned. "Were you aware the dude was the groom? I mean, were you out-of-your-mind-drunk or something?"

Madison wished she had at least plausible deniability. Wouldn't it be great to be able to say she was so drunk she hadn't realized who Tyler was? But she couldn't. "I knew," she confessed. "And I was tipsy, but definitely not drunk."

"So what made you do it? I know your other cousin is a total bitch, but you're not mean or vindictive. Did Georgiana do something bad today? Was kissing the groom a crazy revenge play?"

"Yes and no." Madison covered her face with her hands and shook her head. "Georgiana was her usual nasty self, but nothing out of the ordinary. She didn't say or do anything I haven't heard before… It's just that lately, with everything that's been going on, I haven't been myself."

"Why? What's been going on? What are you talking about?"

"The fight with Alice about Jack… Haley, she *says* she's forgiven me for sleeping with Jack, but she hasn't, not completely, at least, and I miss our friendship so much…"

"Alice!" Haley seemed to have just remembered they had another roommate. "Where is she?"

"Still at the wedding, or getting here. Ethan is giving her a ride; his girlfriend lives near campus."

Haley low-whistled. "Awkward."

"Another thing she can hate me for."

"Come on, Maddie, Alice doesn't hate you."

"I'll agree with you if she doesn't come home tonight." Madison mustered a small smile. "Jack was waiting for her downstairs when I got here, seemed like he'd been there all day…"

"Ah, I didn't see him, think he got her?"

"One can hope."

"Anyway, about today… I know you, Maddie. The fight with Alice wasn't enough to drive you to a make out session with your cousin's groom on their wedding day."

Madison looked away, blushing. "No, but it got me to mull over that period of my life… Freshman year?"

"What about it?"

"Nothing special. I just met a lot of assholes that year who weren't exactly nice to me, and neither was Jack." Madison threw her mug-free hand up before Haley could say anything. "I'm sure he's going to make Alice happy, it's clear he's in love with her, but back then…"

"No prince charming, I get it."

Madison scoffed. "Nowhere near."

"Maddie, you're circling around what's really upset you."

"I'm only saying I was already in a fragile state of mind when David rocked the boat for good."

Madison felt Haley stiffen at the mention of David—her boyfriend Scott's brother.

"How?"

"Our breakup wasn't pretty."

Haley sighed. "Tell me everything."

Madison stared at the wall, gaze unfocused, as a memory of that day danced before her eyes.

***

"I've told you a thousand times I don't want to meet here," David said as he opened his apartment door to find Madison standing on the other side. "Hello" and "come in" apparently forgotten.

"Yeah, but Scott is at my place with Haley, so I thought it'd be okay to hang here for a change," Madison said. "Plus, I didn't want to be there right now."

David finally moved aside to let her in. "Why not?"

"Alice and I had this huge fight. It's all solved in theory, but I'd still rather not be at home."

"You and Alice? Not Haley?"

"No, why would I fight with Haley?"

"No reason, apparently." David sounded annoyed—no, more like disappointed. Madison came closer to hug him, but he shuffled away. "I don't have time for this."

"Why? School's over. You only have to wait for Commencement Day. Are you nervous?"

"No."

Madison fished in her bag for a gift-wrapped book. "This is for you: my graduation present."

David arched an eyebrow as he took the gift. "What is it?"

"A collection of my favorite poems."

David chuckled at first. "Priceless, that's priceless." Then he laughed bitterly. "Can you really be that stupid?"

Madison flushed in mortification. "You don't have to read it if you don't want to."

David threw the book across the room, the wrapping paper tearing as it hit the wall. "I'm not my brother!" he shouted. "I don't care about the words of other tormented souls who've been dead for centuries."

"It's only a present, no need to be such a dick about it."

David pinched his nose. "This isn't working out."

"What isn't?"

"You, us, this."

Tears Madison had fought hard not to shed started to roll down her cheeks. "Why?"

"I can't stand you. All you do is talk, talk, talk"—David mimicked the action with his hand—"all the time. I can stand you only when you're asleep."

"What are you talking about? We've been dating for two months and you never said a thing."

"A mistake, clearly."

"If you hate me so much, why go out with me at all?"

"You had your purpose. Seems it's run out."

"What purpose?"

"Madison, I need you to leave." David pushed past her and reopened the door.

"But—"

"GET OUT!"

***

"I had no idea what to say, Haley, I basically fled the place… It was so humiliating," Madison said, concluding her tale. "It made me feel… I don't know, worthless."

"You're not worthless," Haley hissed, pulling her into a tighter hug.

There was a fury in her friend's words that made Madison lift her head to look Haley in the eye. "What's up with you? You seem angrier than I am."

"It's David. I *hate* him."

"Yeah, well… You tried to warn me about him. My bad I didn't listen."

"No, you did nothing wrong. He's a jerk."

"Yeah, but I'm not such an angel, remember? Anyway, between him, the Alice/Jack drama, and my family… I lost it today."

"Tell me how it started, precisely."

"With a ketchup spill." Madison chuckled bitterly. "So ridiculous! During the buffet, I had ketchup on my fingers after eating a slider burger… I was looking for a napkin when I almost bumped into the bride. Georgiana was a mean bitch as always. She said something about me being a pig and how I was fatter than her even if she was three months pregnant." Madison closed her eyes. "At that moment I hated her, Haley. I'd never felt a loathing so strong. She made me sick. I wanted to grab her by the hair and smash her face into the mayonnaise dip."

Haley scoffed. "She sounds precious enough."

"But of course I didn't do anything; I just stood there and let her walk all over me. I smiled, cleaned my hands on a napkin, and got back to my table, which, being a bridesmaid, was the same as the bride and groom. For the entire lunch, I had to stomach Georgiana ranting on about how perfect her life was… Tyler was seated right in front of me and seemed equally rattled by Georgiana's ramblings. I caught him looking at me more than once and I was happy about it. It was like my little secret revenge against Georgiana. I was thinking, 'You might've forced him to marry you by getting pregnant accidentally-on-purpose, but he doesn't love you.'"

"So you *wanted* to sleep with the groom?"

"Not really, I was happy with him eye-flirting with me, but then things got out of control. By the end of the meal I just needed to get out. I couldn't stand Georgiana a second longer, so I walked away to get some air. I was hiding in the garden behind a hedge when Tyler found me. He was being all nice and cute and charming, and I thought, 'Screw Georgiana.' I wanted to hurt her. I wanted to hurt myself and all my family… It's hard to explain. I knew I was doing something wrong and self-destructive, but I wanted to do it anyway."

"And all of this because of David?"

"David, Georgiana, Alice, Jack, my life in general…" *The fact that I'm in love with your boyfriend,* Madison added inside her head. "Your pick."

"But in the end, nothing unrepairable happened," Haley said. "I mean, it could've been horrible, but it wasn't. Vicky seemed more worried than mad."

"You didn't see the glare in Ethan's eyes. He's never talking to me again."

"I'm sure that's not true. He'll come around if you leave him time to process." Haley squeezed her hand supportively. "He probably has no idea what a bitch his sister can be. Vicky will give him a reality check."

"Mmm, I wouldn't be so sure. Ethan has such a blind spot when it comes to Georgiana."

"But not Vicky?"

"No, she loves her sister, but can still see Georgiana's many flaws. Vicky is the only person in my family I feel close to."

Haley grimaced. "I'm sorry I gave her such a hard time."

"Thanks for being my champion, by the way." Madison smiled at her friend. "I'm sure your protective attitude let Vicky know her nut-job of a cousin was in good hands."

"You're not a nut job."

"Wish I could believe you."

"But you had a hell of a day. Why don't you try to sleep it off?"

"Will you stay with me?"

"Sure, let me just get changed."

Haley went to her room and came back wearing a pastel rainbow unicorn onesie covered in little multicolor stars. She snuggled under the covers next to Madison and comforted her until she fell into a dreamless sleep.

Four

Alice

Alice woke up smiling. Even if her brain was still half-unconscious, the joy was too strong not to seep through all the layers of her mind. She was so used to waking up being the hard part, the moment when she'd have to remember it had all been a dream. That she wasn't Jack's girlfriend, that they hadn't made love all night, and that he'd never see her that way.

Not today.

Today reality surpassed all fantasies. Her toes curled under the sheets as memories of how they'd spent the night IRL flashed before her eyes. *Yeah, definitely better than every dream could ever hope to be.* For a brief moment she doubted herself; could that really all have happened? Slowly, Alice lifted her lids, eyes focusing at once on the very naked proof that, *yes*, it had been real.

Jack was lying on the bed next to her. Head tilted to the side on the pillow, dark hair ruffled in all directions, and not a sock on his body. She ran her fingertips down the length of his collarbone and arm, all the way to his wrist and back up. She needed to touch as well as see before she could let herself believe Jack was in love with her after they'd been just friends for three years.

A pang of fear made her chest contract. How would their relationship change now? How would they transition into being boyfriend and girlfriend? Would everything be different? Better? Worse? Would sex ruin everything?

Her mental rant was interrupted when Jack opened one eyelid to peek at her sideways. "Ice, I can hear you thinking too much."

"I'm not."

Jack turned sideways to stare at her properly, elbow bent on the pillow, head propped on his hand. "So you weren't getting all inside your head worrying about how our friendship is ruined forever, and how we're doomed, and wondering how long before we break up?"

"No?"

"Good." He pushed a lock of hair away from her face. "Because we're never breaking up."

"How can you be so sure?"

"I love you."

Alice's insides melted. It wasn't the first time he'd told her, but the words were still so new on his lips. She reached up to touch his face, again wanting to make sure he was real and not just a dream. "I love you, too," she whispered back.

Jack pulled her into his arms. "Now that you're mine, I'm never letting you go, Ice. Deal?"

"Deal." Alice giggled. "But at some point, you'll have to let me go home."

"Why?"

Alice pointed to the floor, where her cocktail dress from the wedding lay in a pool of blush chiffon. "As lovely as that dress is, I can't go around all day wearing it."

Jack's mouth curled at the corners. "Fine by me. I prefer you naked anyway."

"You have a roommate," Alice chided. "And I need to check on Blue. Remember the little guy who introduced us?"

"Remind me to buy him some expensive bunny treats." Jack smiled. "Can you have breakfast in a cocktail dress?"

Alice's stomach grumbled in reply. "Starbucks' patrons don't judge, and I'm starving."

She'd eaten plenty at the wedding, but they'd skipped dinner altogether last night. They'd been too busy doing… what Jack was starting to do now…

Alice's body tingled under his touch, and with a playful smile, she said, "Now, now. Just because you got lucky once…"

"Oh, yeah?"

Alice squirmed under his gaze.

Jack's grin was wicked. "So it was just a one-off?"

Whatever sassy reply Alice was trying to come up with was silenced by Jack's lips. Oh, gosh, he was *so* going to get lucky any time he wanted.

***

Alice was fighting hard not to sing her joy to the world as she unlocked the door of her apartment. With a full belly, the phantom of Jack's lips all over her body, the more visible trail of beard burns all over her face and neck, and the echo of those simple, life-changing words—*I love you*—ringing in her ears, Alice was walking on a cloud and sporting a smile so wide her cheeks ached.

The smile, however, was short-lived. It died on her lips as she spotted Haley's anxious expression. Her roommate was standing in the living room holding her chin with one hand in a pensive pose. When she heard Alice come in, instead of saying *"Hello"* Haley pressed a finger to her lips and pointed at Madison's door with her other hand.

"What's going on?" Alice whispered. Haley closed the distance between them and made to push her back out the door, but Alice resisted. "Wait, I have to get changed and take a shower."

"The shower can wait," Haley whispered back. "We need to talk. Put something on and meet me on the roof. Please be quiet, I don't want Madison to wake up."

Begrudgingly, Alice shuffled into her room and changed into a pair of sweatpants and a T-shirt. She checked Blue's cage. It had already been cleaned and the bunny fed. Well, even if they didn't let her shower, at least her roommates were good for something.

That's when Alice remembered Madison had come home from the wedding in tears yesterday and she'd left Haley to deal with the mess, not sparing the matter a second thought until now. She hadn't even texted Madison to ask her how she was. And from Haley's urgency, the issue was far from solved.

I'm a horrible friend.

Now filled with worry, Alice hurried to the rooftop.

"What's going on?" she asked as soon as she set foot outside.

Haley turned to face her, eyes positively murderous. "I'm going to kill David Williams. I hate him, Alice, I hate him so much."

"Why? What happened? What did he do?"

Haley sighed. "I've been authorized to tell you everything, since Madison wants you to know, but she's not in the right state of mind to repeat the whole story…"

The more Haley talked, the more Alice started to connect all the dots from the previous day and weeks. The blue shadows under Madison's eyes.

Her pale face, newly cynical view on weddings, and general subdued attitude. Madison pretending the breakup with David had been unimportant, and her refusal to discuss it. Alice had blamed Madison's sudden reticence on their argument over Jack, but deep down she'd known something else had to have happened. It seemed David Williams had happened! And one of her best friends—*yours truly*—abandoning Madison at a time of need had happened. Even after she'd learned about their breakup, Alice hadn't asked, because her pride and heart were still sore after discovering Jack and Madison had had a one-night stand in freshman year. And Haley had probably been too clueless as usual to notice—they usually had to spell things out for her where people's feelings were concerned. Haley could talk to robots, but she found people much harder to read.

As Haley wrapped up the full story, more pieces fell into place. Madison's sudden disappearance from the wedding the day before. Ethan, Vicky, and Rose confabulating in a close circle. Ethan's homicidal expression when he looked at Tyler. And the groom's pale and frazzled appearance.

What. A. Mess. No wonder Ethan was giving me attitude yesterday, *Alice thought. At least now it made sense.*

"…And then there's Scott," Haley concluded.

"Madison likes him more than she's letting on, doesn't she?"

Well, ding-dong, Haley. That took you long enough to grasp.

"Mmm," was all Alice mumbled, not wanting to confirm Haley's fears, regardless of how well-founded they might be.

"Mmm?" Haley turned toward her, crossing her arms over her chest. "Is that all you have to say?"

No, *Alice thought*. I want to tell you how happy I am. How crazily, stupidly in love I feel. I want to savor the joy at least for twenty-four hours without being pulled into more drama.

Alice chided her inner self for being so selfish. One of her friends was in pain and all messed up. No matter what Madison had failed to confess, she'd always been there to support Alice through every Jack crisis. They had spent endless movie nights in whenever Jack had a new date and Alice was too depressed to go out. And Madison hated watching TV, she only loved books.

"We have to do something," Haley insisted.

"Yeah, but…" Alice pulled her hair up into a ponytail. "What *can* we do? I mean, other than being around and being supportive?"

"I don't know, Alice. I feel so guilty. She's in love with Scott, isn't she?"

"I can't honestly say," Alice said vaguely.

Haley threw her a no-bullshit look.

"Okay," Alice conceded. "I suspect she's more into Scott than she's letting on."

"Wonderful!" Haley pressed her hands to her temples.

"Hey, it's not your fault. You don't have to feel guilty about dating him."

"But how could I not? I'm his girlfriend. Remember how much you used to hate Jack's girlfriends? How can Madison stand to live with me?"

"First, those are a lot of questions, and second, I'm sure Madison doesn't hate you."

"Would you not hate me? Just a few weeks ago you wanted to claw her eyes out for sleeping with Jack, *once*, three years ago. And I've been with Scott for the past six months, right in her face! And I'm not even considering giving him up because I'm just so in love with him… but then, it's impossible not to feel guilty about how happy I am."

Alice nudged Haley shoulder-to-shoulder. "So is Scott *the* one?"

Her friend smiled. "I suspect he might be. I've never felt this way for anyone."

"Not even for the infamous masked dude from last summer?"

"Please don't remind me about that." Haley hid her face behind her hands. "I dance with a masked stranger at a party, kiss him, never learn his name, and spend the next six months obsessing over him. How lame is that?"

"Sounded pretty romantic when you were telling us the story." Alice started talking using what she called a "movie trailer" voice. "A lonely dame at a ball rescued by a mysterious masked gentleman who sweeps her off her feet, leading her in a passionate dance—"

"He was a horrible dancer."

"It's the thought that counts." Alice continued talking in her movie voice. "A romantic stroll in the gardens under a thousand fairy lights, and then, at the stroke of midnight, an epic kiss…"

Haley laughed at her theatrics, but said, "It wasn't midnight, I'm no Cinderella, and it's the dude who fled the ball without telling me his name. Sometimes I even wonder if that night was real. You know when something seems so 'too good to be true' that you ask yourself if it wasn't all a dream?"

Haley had just described how Alice had woken up that morning, and she couldn't suppress the little smirk that escaped her lips. "I know."

Haley caught the smile and flashed a grin back. "Tell me, Miss Brown, are those beard burns all over your face?"

Alice couldn't keep it inside any longer, she told Haley everything. How Jack had waited for her in front of their building, how he'd told her he was in love with her, and how they'd spent the night and the best part of the morning.

"Great!" Haley scoffed sarcastically. "So we're both the happiest we've ever been and our best friend is at an all-time low. Alice, I love Scott so much… and he loves me back… a-and I don't know how to shield Madison from all that."

"For one, we don't rub our happiness in her face."

"And for two?"

"We have to avoid becoming two of those cheesy couples that do things only in pairs. We have to keep going out with a wider group of people—singles and couples—and include Madison as much as possible. And when she has a low day and needs a girls' night in, we tell the beloved boyfriends to beat it."

"And you think that will be enough?"

Alice shrugged. "It's the best we can do; we can't fix her love life for her. When Madison's ready, she'll find the right guy. In the meantime, our job is to be around as much as possible and to force Madison to be social."

"She likes parties more than I do."

"True, but what guys do you usually pick up at parties?"

"The wrong kind. Gotcha."

"Anyway, there won't be many parties, at least for a while." Alice sighed. "Not with almost everyone gone for the summer."

"Right. Only the best are left." Haley smiled, staring at the Boston skyline in the distance. "I could never spend a whole summer home."

"Me neither, I'd be bored out of my mind."

"And also lovesick over Jack."

"Especially lovesick over Jack." Alice flashed her friend a megawatt smile. "So how's your schedule for summer break? Are you going to be super busy?"

"Nah." Haley toyed with a lock of hair, curling it around her fingers. "I'm taking three summer courses, but I should be able to stick around a lot. You?"

"Same for me. I'm doing an internship at a pharmaceutical company downtown, but it's mornings only." Alice grinned. "Jack applied for the same program without telling me, you know, when we weren't speaking…"

"I like his style."

"Yeah, me too. You know what Madison is doing?"

"A literary research project for her department."

"And Scott?"

"He applied for a few internships, something to do with pre-med school. But no answers so far, I think. We haven't really discussed it yet."

"Okay, so everyone will be here for the

summer," Alice said. "Now that we have a plan, can I go shower?"

"Yeah, thanks for the pep talk." Haley pulled her into a hug and added jokingly, "Now you can go wash Jack off."

They both laughed and stumbled toward the elevator, still hugging each other. They were a team; they could solve any problem if they stuck together.

Five

Haley

Haley spent Sunday at home with her roommates. They baked cookies together, and Haley and Alice made an effort to avoid any boy talk. The strain was clear on Alice's part; she was bursting with happiness and it was obvious she had to check herself not to smile and hum love tunes under her breath 24/7. For her part, Madison put on a brave face and let them organize the day for her.

But being a good friend had meant ditching her boyfriend for most of the weekend. So as she knocked on Scott's door early on Monday afternoon, Haley was super eager to jump into his arms.

When he came to open the door, Haley's breath caught in her chest.

That face. Those eyes. That mouth.

Despite the fact that they'd been dating for six months, he still had that effect on her. Today he was wearing a bright blue tank top that made his muscled arms stand out, a pair of white basketball shorts, and his feet were bare on the wooden floor. His dirty blonde hair was already streaked golden from the first real sun of summer, and he'd never looked better.

Scott smiled. "Hey."

The smile brightened his entire face, from his sexy lips to his emerald green eyes.

"Hey, you," Haley breathed when Scott hugged her.

He smelled like he always did: soapy, manly, delicious. But when Haley pressed her face into Scott's chest, guilt suddenly flared through her. Haley was here in his arms, and Madison was at home, *alone*. They were in love with the same guy, and that was a problem without a solution. One of them would always end up being hurt. Unless, of course, one of them stopped loving him.

But how could you not love Scott? It was inconceivable. He was gorgeous, smart, kind, and sexy as hell. He was also a bookworm like Madison. They'd been sharing the same Lit classes for years. Haley could just picture her best friend adoring Scott from a distance, too shy to talk to him. She was equally glad and sad Madison had never mustered the courage to speak to Scott. If she had, Scott could've been Madison's boyfriend now; they had so much in common. They both were words people, whereas Haley preferred numbers.

But, hey, opposites attract.

And as guilty as Haley felt, there was no way

she would ever give up Scott.

He pulled her into the apartment and shut the door, his lips slowly making their way from her neck to her mouth.

"It's only been a day, but I've missed you," Scott whispered in her ear.

Haley mumbled something back, too distracted by the cute, tiny freckles scattered all over his shoulders. All she wanted to do now was take off his top and feel that hard chest pressed against hers as she dug her nails into his muscled back. She started kissing the freckles, one by one. And Scott must've been a mind reader, because in a swift move he took off the tank top, draping it over his other shoulder.

"Easy, tiger," Haley joked, pushing him toward his room all the same.

He flashed her a grin. "From the way you're looking at me, I thought you were the tiger."

Yeah, that was exactly how she felt. Like a hungry cat ready to pounce.

Haley kicked the door shut and pushed Scott onto the bed. Then she almost jumped into his arms, losing herself in the kisses of the boy she loved so much. And at that moment there wasn't space for anyone else in her mind. There were only Scott and his kisses.

***

The guilt waited until a couple of hours later to sneak back into Haley's mind and start whispering in her ear about how selfish she was for being so utterly happy.

"Are you sure you're okay?" Scott asked.

They were cozied up on his bed. Haley had stolen his tank top—she loved wearing his clothes—which reached almost to her knees.

Basketball players are tall. Haley winked to herself for dating one who, at present, was left shirtless next to her.

Haley shuffled across the bed and dropped her head onto that beautiful, smooth-skinned chest. "Yes, sorry." She kissed one of his flat-muscled pectorals. "I'm just a little distracted."

A little distracted. That's one way of putting it.

Haley was positively torn between two loyalties. On one side stood Scott. She wanted to tell him everything, not to keep secrets from him. But then there was Madison. Haley couldn't expose her friend's feelings to him. If the roles were reversed, Haley would be humiliated by his knowledge. Neither could she discuss how disgusting his brother's behavior toward Madison had been when David had dumped her. She had to put Madison's need for privacy before anything else; her best friend was fragile and needed to be protected. But it still sucked not being able to tell her boyfriend why she was in such a bad mood.

The front door slammed shut and Haley jolted in Scott's arms.

"Sounds like my charming roommate is home," Scott said.

The risk of bumping into David had been a calculated one when Haley had asked Scott to meet at his place. Better than Madison running into Scott at their apartment. Plus, Haley couldn't make love to Scott with Madison in the adjoining room. It would break whatever was left of her friend's heart.

"When is he moving out?" Haley asked. "I mean, isn't school over? Shouldn't he get on with his life, get a job somewhere, or something?"

Scott sighed. "I'm afraid that's not David's plan."

"What do you mean?"

"He's doing a summer internship at an investment bank in downtown Boston, and he's starting his MBA at Harvard Business School in the fall."

"So he'll be here for another two years."

"Yep."

"And he's not moving out…"

"Nope. But at least he won't be on the basketball team any longer. I'll see him less than ever and so will you especially…"

It'd better be that way.

Haley wasn't sure she could control her rage around David. There was something in him that made her go to extremes. She'd never thought she'd be able to loathe someone, *really hate*, but David had proved her wrong.

"…Would you want to go?"

Where?

Scott had kept on talking and was now looking at her expectantly. He wore a little frown, but was trying hard to smile as if he wanted to be casual about what he was asking, when in fact it was something he cared deeply about. But *what* was he asking?

"Go where? I'm sorry, I got lost in thought again." Haley forced herself to stop twirling her hair and pay attention. "Where are you going?"

"Damn, you really are distracted." Scott's face fell with disappointment. "Are you sure you don't want to tell me what it's about?"

"I'm sure," Haley said, and made a move-on-with-what-you-were-saying gesture while squeezing his hand to show him her worries did not concern their relationship.

Scott rolled his eyes, but he let it go. "I said that you'll have to see even less of my brother if you come to California with me this summer."

Haley's chest contracted with sudden fear. "Since when are you spending the summer in California?" Haley disentangled herself from

Scott's arms to stare at him.

"I wasn't until this morning."

"What happened this morning?"

"I got this." Scott handed her his phone, an email opened on the screen.

Haley quickly skimmed the text. It was an official acceptance notice for Scott to shadow a certain Dr. Kendrick Allen, a neurological surgeon.

"I know it's last minute," Scott said as Haley kept reading the details of the email. The internship started on June 20—*only two weeks from today*—and ended on August 26, the week before the fall term started. *Two months without Scott.* "But I never expected Dr. Allen to accept my application. This guy is like the best in his field, he's leading this revolutionary research program on neuro—"

"I can't come," Haley interrupted him. "You know I'm taking summer courses."

"I thought you were just considering it. You never told me you actually enrolled." Scott's eyes widened. "Summer School, huh?"

Haley stared at the bedspread, her finger picking at a loose thread. She knew Summer School sounded uncool. "I like the different crowd." She shrugged. "And there's always interesting people from all over the world with all these unique backgrounds and coding experience."

Oh, hell. Did that come out as lame and geeky as it sounded in my head?

Scott lifted her chin with a finger. "Well, that settles it, then. I'm not going."

"But it's an incredible opportunity."

"I have a backup internship in Boston. I never thought Dr. Allen would pick me."

"Because he's the best."

"He is, but the doctor here in Boston is amazing too."

"But not *as* great." Haley sighed. She didn't want Scott to go. But for him to lose such a once-in-a-lifetime opportunity because of her... "Two months isn't a long time," she lied.

Two months without him would stretch on for an eternity.

"Haley Thomas, I'm not going anywhere without you," Scott declared. "I love you, and I don't want to spend a single day apart. End of story."

A warm fuzz threatened to turn Haley's inside to jelly. Scott's gaze was so intense, and he sounded so sure. She stared at the phone still clutched in her hand. Scott had until Friday to accept—or refuse. The offer would stand for four more days.

"Don't reply today," she said. He was about to protest, but she stopped him. "Please, take all the time you have to think about it. I want you to be sure. An opportunity like this is too important for you, for your future career. Take at least a couple of days to think it over."

"I will, but I'm not moving to California without you."

***

Dating varsity basketball players had its cons. Haley would've loved to spend the entire evening with Scott, but tonight he had to go meet a few of his teammates for an outdoor basketball game. Last winter, basketball had been the silent third wheel in their relationship and even now that the official Harvard Crimson team training had stopped for summer break, the game was still a huge part of Scott's life. He spent almost as much time training now as during the regular season, and never missed an opportunity to play.

So, after spending every last possible second with Scott, Haley was running late. She'd just left his apartment and was hurrying home, wondering why phones had the special ability to lose themselves inside a woman's bag.

Haley rummaged again in her maxi bag, but her hands kept coming in contact with all sorts of different things; everything but a phone. And she needed to call her mom ASAP. She could picture her mother already staring at her smartphone, fretting as she waited for Haley's call.

Miranda Thomas was the techiest of her parents and the one who could always be relied upon to pick up whenever Haley called. She would then put the call on speaker for Haley's dad to take part. Weekly calls were Haley's special ritual with her mom and dad. She rang them every Monday and Friday night—and tried to never miss an appointment.

Haley rattled her bag and attempted another blind search, but with all the stuff cluttered inside, she couldn't find the phone. Especially not while she was speed-walking across campus.

Frustrated, she stopped near a bench and, with a sigh, knelt next to it and up-ended the overfilled bag onto the seat. When something disappeared into the folds of her maxi bag, there was no other way of luring it out. But even after a forensic examination of all the objects scattered on the bench seat, her phone was still MIA.

A flashback of taking the phone out of her bag to check her texts and dropping it on Scott's nightstand shot through Haley's head. Unfortunately, there was no follow-up memory of taking the phone from the night table and putting it back into the bag.

Haley groaned, swatting the bench.

The phone was at Scott's apartment, and Scott

was at a game that would last at least two hours, maybe more. But Haley had to call her mom—she checked her watch—*right now.*

This left only one solution. After all, the other Williams brother *was* at home. Haley groaned again. She really didn't want to confront David. Not today. Not ever. But what other choice did she have? She could hurry home and Skype her parents instead, but the thought of her phone being alone in the same house as David Williams gave her the creeps. And since her mom would probably call her way before she could get home and in front of a computer, David would know the phone was there because he'd hear it ringing.

Shoving everything back into her bag with a sweep of her arm, Haley got up and hurried back toward Scott's house.

Six

Haley

"I forgot my phone," Haley said, skipping the pleasantries and barging into the apartment past David.

"Hello, Sunshine," he said, using his usual mocking tone. "Would you like to come in?"

"I'm just picking up my phone and then I'm gone."

"You mean this?"

Haley stopped halfway toward Scott's room and turned around. David stood there looking at her with an arrogant, self-satisfied face that demanded to be slapped. An infuriating lopsided grin was stamped on his cruel lips. He must've picked up her phone from somewhere because he was wiggling it tantalizingly between his thumb and index finger.

She marched back to where he was standing. "Give it back." Haley made to grab the phone, but he raised his arms over his head, way out of her reach.

Damn basketball players and their being super tall—*or ex-basketball players, in this case.*

"Say please," David taunted.

Haley gave up the fight to reach the phone and stared him down. "David, stop it. I need to call my mom; I don't want her to worry."

"Miranda? Looovely lady."

"How do you know my mother's name?"

"Before you got here, she'd already called three times and, as you said, we wouldn't want the lovely Miranda to get worried, so I picked up and acted voicemail. You're welcome."

"You looked into my phone?"

David scoffed. "Don't worry; your lovey-dovey, emoji-filled texts with my brother would be too boring for me to spy on."

"I want my phone back."

He took a step forward so that now he was towering over her, crowding her space, his gaze intense. "Say. Please."

A familiar scent Haley couldn't quite place—one associated with a positive memory—filled her nostrils. Confused, Haley backed away instinctively. "Stop doing that."

"Doing what?" David asked, acting all innocent.

"The flirty eyes thing, and the charming act... I want nothing to do with you."

His eyes flared bluer, if that was even possible. "Now," he said, tossing her the phone. Haley caught it and quickly texted her mom to say she'd call her later. All the while David kept talking.

"There's really no need to be rude. If you're mad you can't withstand my charms, that's your problem, darling."

"Your charms?" Haley hissed, pressing Send and fixing her narrowed gaze on him. "What charms? Yeah, you've pretty eyes and a pretty face, but that's it. You're mean and cruel for no reason. The way you hurt Madison makes me sick, you—"

"Your friend is just another stupid girl in love with my soppy brother. Madison didn't care about me enough for me to really hurt her. She used me as a rebound, same as I did her. But speaking of hurting Blondie…" David snapped his fingers, then pointed one at her. "I bet your relationship with dear old Scotty is doing more damage to her right now than I ever could."

A blow too close to home. Haley was at a loss for words.

"Ooh." David smiled, satisfied. "Seems I've touched a sore point. I apologize, Sunshine."

Rage flared in Haley's chest. "You don't even try to deny you used her. How can you be so arrogant after everything you've done? You should be ashamed of yourself."

"You confuse me for someone who cares about your opinion, little miss 'I like to judge.'" His next words came out in a low hiss. "None of this matters to me. None of it."

"Then why do you even bother to tease me all the time?"

"Oh, that?" David asked, his voice mocking again. "That's just for fun. I enjoy watching how hard you try to deny the obvious chemistry between us."

"There's no chemistry between us," Haley spat. "I wouldn't touch you with a ten-foot pole if you were the last guy on earth."

"Might be too late for that, my dear."

"What do you mean?"

David started walking toward her, slowly, deliberately. Haley backed away until her shoulders came in contact with the living room wall. David stopped a few steps short of where she was standing and covered the top half of his face with his hands. He lifted the index finger of each hand to show only his eyes through the narrow gap, giving the impression he was looking at her through a mask.

And then he bowed.

***

"Would you do me the honor of this dance?"

The guy bowing in front of Haley was staring up at her through an elaborate black mask. His eyes were a dazzling electric blue and the corner of his mouth was turned up in a lopsided grin that promised danger.

"But of course." Haley did a coy little curtsy and took the stranger's hand. "Mister…?"

"Giving you my name would defy the purpose of us wearing masks," the man said, taking her hand and straightening his back. He was remarkably tall, a good full head taller than Haley.

"My gentle sir, you find me at a disadvantage," she said, keeping up the pretense of speaking like gents and dames while he led her toward the dance floor. "How is it fair when my face is practically bare and yours almost entirely covered?"

Haley's mask for the Venetian Masquerade Ball consisted of a few strategically placed stick-on Swarovski crystals scattered around her eyes. But the stranger's mask covered the majority of his face, leaving only his lips visible. And those sparkly blue eyes.

He leaned forward and whispered in her ear, "Then I'm all the luckier for it."

If the costume party had been dull up until the mysterious man's appearance—and definitely not worth the investment in her rented princess gown or the ticket's cost—it seemed the night could still turn around.

Keeping at the edges of the dancing crowd, they started swirling in time with the music. Neither of them had a clear idea of what they were doing, but Haley hoped her long skirt made enough of a show to cover for their poor dancing skills. Not that she cared much, anyway; she was too entranced by the blue eyes of the man leading her so inexpertly in what had officially become the most romantic dance of her life.

Not being able to see the guy's face was both enticing and infuriating. He could be anyone and no one. And the only detail the mask didn't leave to the imagination—his full lips—didn't help steady Haley's breath. A hot flush warmed her skin; she had become too sensitive to the touch of one of his hands on the small of her back. And to his other hand holding hers, to the way sharp electric tingles shot down her arm from where their skin touched.

"I've never seen eyes as green as yours," he said.

Haley wanted to reply that the blue of his was no joke either, but it seemed corny to repeat the same compliment he'd just paid her. "You have pretty eyes, too," she said, almost out of breath.

His gaze was so intense it was squeezing the air out of Haley's lungs. They didn't say much afterward; in fact, they didn't speak at all. Haley and her masked stranger stared wordlessly into each other's eyes, green into blue, while they kept doing a poor impression of a waltz.

Haley wasn't able to explain the force of the insta-connection, the way it made her pulse race and her breath short. The music, the costumes, the elegant hall; it all seemed to disappear, reducing Haley's world to those blue eyes and full lips and the thousand faces that could be hiding under the black mask.

Maybe love at first sight was a thing. Even if it turned out she had no idea who this man was, she still felt an ease, a sense of belonging, that she'd hardly ever experienced with any of her exes.

Distracted by her own thoughts, Haley stepped on the stranger's toes.

He winced under the mask and said, "What do you say we take a stroll outside? It's getting scorching hot in here." He rolled a finger on the inside of his shirt's collar. "And we've demonstrated our awful dancing skills enough for one night."

Haley swatted him playfully. "Who are you calling an awful dancer?"

He smiled wickedly and offered her his elbow. Haley linked their arms together and followed him outside, where the temperature was a bit cooler thanks to a crisp evening breeze abating the late summer heat.

The villa where the party was being hosted resembled more a European palace out of a fairy tale than a countryside mansion in Massachusetts. With its imposing size, light brick architecture, turrets, and large windows, it was more castle than house. And its gardens were just as stylish, a mix of flower beds and shrubs organized in symmetric geometrical patterns and lit with a thousand fairy lights.

There was a small gazebo in the center of the garden, a wrought iron structure covered in white roses silhouetted against the dark night sky. Without speaking, they both headed toward the flowery cage. It seemed like a good place to talk—or not talk.

When they stopped underneath the arch, the tension in Haley's body spiked. She felt edgier than the first time she'd kissed someone.

"You make me nervous," she told the stranger.

He held both her hands close to his chest as he faced her. "Good nervous or bad nervous?"

"Good, I think."

He tilted his head at her questioningly, and Haley started to over-talk. "I don't know your name or what your face looks like, but I feel like I've known you forever. Can you at least tell me if you're from around here? Will I see you again after tonight?"

"I go to school in Cambridge. I'm about to start senior year."

"Me too. You go to Harvard? What's your major?"

"Shh..." He pressed a finger to her lips. "So many questions..."

Haley kissed the finger in what she hoped was a sensual gesture, then guided his hand down to rest on her waist. "So little answers..."

The charming stranger joined both his hands behind her back and pulled her against his body. Less than an inch separated their faces now. For the first time, Haley's nostrils filled with his scent—a mix of sun-kissed skin and a citrus aroma, bergamot or orange. A fragrance that was woody, citrusy, and salty at the same time. It made her think of a sunny day on a boat in the middle of the Mediterranean. It's what Haley imagined all those male models from D&G perfume commercials must smell like.

The mysterious man spared her the time to take another ragged breath before he closed the distance between them. Their lips finally connected, and despite them not dancing anymore, the world still seemed to spin around them. She clung to him—to his chest, to his shoulders, to his neck—the only firm point in a dizzy, swaying universe. The kiss didn't start softly or tentatively; like everything else between them so far, it was forceful right from the beginning. Not just intense, but deep, powerful, passionate… and somewhat more meaningful than every kiss Haley had ever given or received. In the arms of this mysterious man, Haley felt helpless and secure at the same time.

When he let go of her mouth, he left a trail of gentle kisses down her neck, then brushed a thumb down her cheek and over her lower lip. Haley wasn't sure she was made of flesh and bones any longer; she was worried her body might melt under the stranger's touch.

She was about to pull his face down to hers once more when angry shouts and a crashing sound reached them from inside the house. Haley turned to check what the commotion was and caught sight of several security guards running after another impressively tall guy. The "fugitive" was heading in their direction.

"Oh-ho," the masked stranger said, "looks like we've been found out."

"Why? You know that guy?"

"Yep, we came together."

"What did you do?"

"We aren't exactly invited guests to this party."

"How did you even get in??" Haley asked.

"Climbed over the fence. And now I have to go."

"But—" Haley began. *Her mystery man cut her off by pulling her into a passionate but hurried kiss. She was still collecting herself when he winked, stepped away, and walked backward toward the gate.*

The runaway friend had now almost reached them; as he raced toward the gazebo, he yelled, "We gotta beat it, my man!"

The masked stranger bowed one more time to Haley, wearing that impossibly sexy, wicked grin, and then he was running away.

"Wait!" she shouted as she watched him go. "You haven't even told me your name..."

Still running, the unknown man who had stolen Haley's heart turned his head and smiled again, his lips forming an answer, the sound of which got lost among the shouts of the security guards chasing after him...

Seven

Haley

A year later, as Haley relived the memory as if in slow motion, the lost answer became suddenly clear. Finally, she was able to read the word on the stranger's lips… David.

"It was you?" she asked the real-life David standing in front of her.

"In the flesh." He bowed lower, before removing his hands from his face and straightening up.

Time seemed to stop for Haley as they stood immobile facing each other, blue eyes locked on green ones. Haley didn't know what to do, say, or even what to think. She was too busy trying to breathe normally and ignore the electricity filling the air. Thank goodness her back was already pressed against the wall; she leaned on it for support.

David couldn't be the masked stranger, he couldn't. Oh, but he was… there was no denying it. The startling blue of his eyes was the same. Haley lowered her gaze slightly… and his full lips were the same. How had she never noticed before?

"Don't look at me like that." He took a step

forward. "You know I can't resist you when you do."

Haley moved her lips to voice a reply, but her mouth had gone dry. The hard drive of her mind had just received too much conflicting information; it was in override, and her brain couldn't compute anymore.

"S-stay r-right where you are," she stammered.

David took another step forward.

"David, no."

Haley tried to dodge him by shifting to the side, but he was quicker. "No?" He grabbed Haley's shoulders and pressed her harder against the wall—his sun-kissed and salty fragrance invaded her nostrils. "Tell me you don't want to kiss me again. Tell me that night didn't stay with you for a long time, because it sure did stay with me."

Yeah, it had. But it didn't matter now. This was David. *David.* The same guy who had hurt Madison so badly, the same brother Scott hated so much. He was the same D-bag who enjoyed playing games with other people's feelings. He had said it himself: this was all a joke to him.

"Back off," she shouted, pushing him away with all her force. "What happened that night changes nothing."

Stumbling backward, he laughed, full of scorn. "Tell yourself whatever you like."

Haley straightened the strap of her bag over her shoulder and walked past him, heading for the door. "I'm leaving."

"All right, Sunshine, but please try not to dream too wildly about me tonight."

With one last glare, Haley flung the door open and fled the apartment.

***

"So the dude in the black mask was David?" Alice asked from her spot on the couch next to Haley. "Like, for real?" Her roommate was still reeling in shock from the revelation—just like Haley, no matter that she'd had a couple of extra hours to digest the news.

Haley fluffed a pillow and leaned back, hugging it to her chest while she tucked her knees neatly under her chin. The position prevented her from nodding, so she mumbled a "yep" back.

Madison was perched on the armchair in front of them, equally shocked. She was staring at Haley wide-eyed, apparently too weirded out to speak.

"Wow, I mean, just whoa," Alice said, fluttering her hands. "Why did you think he waited so long to tell you?"

Ah, that was a very good question. Haley had no clue what the answer might be.

"What if he was waiting for the moment it'd hurt the most?" Madison spoke for the first time since Haley had got home and told her best friends of the dreadful discovery. "Did something happen between you and Scott?"

"No," Haley said. "Nothing out of the ordinary. I have no idea why David chose today of all days to remove the pin from the grenade."

"So," Alice asked tentatively, "is it a grenade?"

"Well," Haley scoffed. "David and I kissed. How do you think Scott is going to take the news?"

"It happened before you even met him. Scott can't get mad about it."

Haley threw Alice an icy stare she hoped sent the message: Yeah, because when you found out Madison had slept with Jack before she even met you, that made you so not care…

Madison caught the stare and blushed.

Alice, too, got the unspoken memo all right and grimaced. "But you didn't know, and it's not like you hid the kiss from Scott on purpose."

"Scott will look at me in a different way. This entire beef between him and David started over another girl they both dated back in high school. So I think Scott is definitely going to mind if his girlfriend happens to have a past with his brother."

"Did David try to steal Scott's girlfriend or

something?" Madison asked.

"It was shadier than that," Haley said. "This French girl, Brigitte, came to their school for an exchange program in her junior year. She was in the same grade as Scott, and a year younger than David."

"Same as you…" Madison interrupted.

"Yeah." Haley didn't like the parallels one bit. "Anyway, apparently she was unbelievably beautiful and had this impossible-to-resist accent…"

Alice raised a skeptical eyebrow.

"…and she was a total bitch," Haley continued. "She started dating David right away, but Scott told me they had like almost every class together, and they talked, and he was in love with her, and things with David weren't going well, blah, blah, blah. Long story short, Miss Brigitte told Scott she'd broken up with David when she hadn't, then started dating him too."

"How's that even possible?" Madison asked.

Haley shrugged. "I only heard Scott's side of the story. She told him it was too soon after her breakup with David for them to date openly."

"Okay," Alice said slowly. "So she kept her relationship with Scott a secret. But if she was still officially dating David, how could Scott not notice?"

"I don't know," Haley said, exasperated. "She

must've been an evil mastermind, making sure she went out with David only when Scott wasn't around."

"For how long?" Alice again.

"I. Don't. Knoooow." Haley was tired of answering all these questions, especially since none of them were bringing her any closer to deciding what to do next. Specifically, how to tell Scott. "Whatever little Scott told me, I had to drag out of him, and already it was harder than a dental extraction."

"Ew." Madison made a gagging impression.

Haley rolled her eyes. "Anyway, I'm not sure *how* it happened. The only certain fact is that at some point David found them together, confronted his brother, and asked Brigitte to choose. She chose Scott, and because Scott kept dating her, David doesn't believe Scott didn't know she'd been cheating on David with him."

Alice low-whistled. "Talk about family intrigue."

"See why I'm not ecstatic history is repeating itself?"

"This is completely different," Alice insisted.

"Totally," Madison agreed. "Hey, do you think David recognized you right away?"

Haley closed her eyes, trying to remember the first time she'd met David—without him wearing a mask, at least. Haley and Alice had been in

Hawaii for Christmas, playing groupies for the Harvard basketball team as Alice had been dating the team's captain, Peter, at the time. That trip had also been when Haley had met Scott. And since Peter and Scott had been sharing a room, Haley had agreed to swap roommates so that Alice and Peter could bunk together. Except reception had confused Scott Williams with David Williams, and they'd sent her to the wrong room. She'd knocked on a door expecting to see Scott, and had found herself staring into David's blue eyes instead. Had he recognized her at once? Haley squeezed her eyes tighter, pressing her hands to her temples. When David had opened the door and found her on his doorstep, all he'd said was: "Hello, again."

Had that *again* meant everything… or nothing at all? Had he simply recognized her from the plane ride? Haley couldn't tell, because immediately after saying hello David had acted like a total jerk, and then Scott had arrived, and then they'd started beating the hell out of each other and trashing the hotel room as they fought.

How didn't I recognize him? Haley asked herself. *His lips, his eyes, his scent…* There'd been a moment when David had pulled her close and held her against his bare chest, just as Scott had turned the corner of the hall and found them talking. David had kept Haley tucked into him for a few long instants to make his brother mad, but he hadn't smelled of citrus and the sea then. He must've used a different soap since they were staying in a hotel and he'd just gotten out of the shower. Or he must've not had the time to put on cologne…

"Hel-lo?" Madison called her back to present.

"Yeah, sorry." Haley rubbed her eyes and opened them. "I'm not sure if he recognized me right away, Maddie. With David, it's always hard to tell what's going on inside his head."

"You know nothing," Alice joked. "You're worse than Jon Snow!"

Haley grabbed a pillow and playfully smothered Alice with it. "You guys aren't helping. I need to decide what to do."

"Hey, I'm innocent here." Alice stole the pillow and positioned it behind her back. "So, is this revelation making you feel any different about David? Does it make you question your relationship with Scott?"

Haley couldn't help but notice the way Madison perked up in her armchair. Almost as if she hoped Haley would say yes. *Sorry, Maddie.* "No, I love Scott," Haley said, looking away.

"Are you sure?" Alice insisted. "When you came back from the Venetian Ball last summer you seemed pretty taken up with masked Dav—"

Madison's super loud ringtone filled the room,

interrupting Alice. "Hello?" she picked up. "No, sure… You do that… No… Yes… I'm on my way." All frenzied by the call, Madison stood up. "Guys, I forgot it's my book club night. I should go or I'll be late." Then she sat back down. "I mean," she added, chewing her lower lip between words. "I can stay if you need me to." And then she started babbling. "It's not like I can't skip one night, even if I'm president of the club. I'm here for you. The chapters we're discussing tonight aren't all that interesting anyway; we're still nowhere near chapter twenty-two or chapter twenty-nine…"

Haley goggled at Alice to check if she had any idea what Madison was rambling about, but her other roommate shrugged and shook her head.

"…but, still, I'm president of the club, and I proposed this month's book—the classic *not* the retelling—so perhaps I should go?"

Madison finally went quiet, even if she kept torturing her lower lip with her teeth.

"Go," Haley said. "I'm fine. I mean, I'm not fine, but you can't do anything about it. And I have Alice to help psychoanalyze me."

"Are you sure?"

"Yep!"

"I'll make it up to you, I promise."

Madison stood up again and, bending at the waist, she pulled Haley into a bone-crushing hug before disappearing into her room to get dressed. She dashed back out all of three minutes later looking adorably crumpled in a frilly short dress with ruffles. Her style was completed by messy hair pinned on top of her head with a pencil, a frayed leather messenger bag strapped across her chest, and giant black glasses covering half her face. She was beautiful in a sexy-but-innocent librarian way, if only she'd realize it. If Madison gained just a dash of self-confidence, she'd be able to get any guy she wanted.

Well, not *any* guy. Not *my* guy.

But there was no reason for Madison not to find a gorgeous, loving, and caring boyfriend.

Haley still couldn't understand why her friend seemed only to fall for the bad boys. Scott being the one decent-guy exception, but also the only guy Madison had never approached.

"I'm going," Madison said. "Call me if you need anything."

Haley smirked. "Aren't cell phones banned from book club meetings?"

Madison's eyes widened, her expression crestfallen.

"I'm joking," Haley said.

"Ah, of course. Well, bye, girls."

Madison blew them each a kiss and then was gone.

After the door clicked shut, Alice waited for all

of two seconds before attacking Haley again with questions. "Now tell me, how do you really feel?"

Haley winced. "I don't knooow." She collapsed theatrically on the couch.

"Mmm… I sense a lie by omission here," Alice insisted.

"Please stay out of my head."

"Please let me in so we can sort out this Williams brothers situation."

"And how do you propose we do that?"

"When I say 'David,' what's your gut feeling?"

The little air pocket Haley felt in her belly was not the reaction she wanted to have after hearing his name. "Sometimes, I'm sort of drawn to him," she confessed. "It's this inexplicable, almost animal thing. He makes me tick, not sure why, because I genuinely dislike him. But whenever I'm near him I'm on edge… and knowing how good a kisser he is doesn't help."

"So you're attracted to him in all his bad-boy glory," Alice said, smirking. "Your body wants him and your mind can't cope."

"Is that even possible?"

"Apparently so." Alice paused for a second before asking the next question. "Have you ever been tempted to… act on this attraction?"

"Hell, no." Haley straightened up. "I'm with Scott, I love Scott. He's the sweetest, most adorable…"

"Hot," Alice suggested.

"…*incredibly hot* boyfriend in the entire world."

"So why are you so worried? If you're not having any existential which-brother-should-I-date doubts, what's the matter?"

"Alice, I know I'm okay. But what about Scott? I don't want to lie to him, but…"

"Lie? Why should you lie?"

"He's going to ask me if I liked the kiss. What should I say?"

"Ah."

"Yeah, ah! What if he starts asking all the wrong questions? Like, did I think about the kiss after it happened…? Should I tell him the truth and say I spent the next six months obsessing over his brother?"

"Err… probably not. You should downplay it a bit."

"In short, lie."

"In short, sugarcoat the truth a little for the greater good?"

"See why I'm not eager to have that conversation?"

Alice pulled Haley's feet onto her lap and started massaging her ankles. "Eager or not, you'd better rip off the Band-Aid. No good can come from waiting."

Haley groaned. "You're so completely right. I hate you."

"Aw, come on, you know you love me. Even when I'm painfully right."

"I do." Haley smacked her lips in a loud air kiss. "Any suggestion on the best way to tell Scott?"

Eight

Madison

"Madison, hey," a familiar male voice called from behind her. "Wait up."

She turned to find Scott waving at her. All the air left her lungs, leaving Madison breathless. Usually, when she saw him, she'd had time to prepare. But to meet him in the street by chance just like that, Madison was caught off guard. He was looking glorious in basketball shorts and a loose tank top, a cool sackpack strapped to his back. Her eyes roamed the length of his bare, muscled arms up to his shoulders, collarbone, chin, mouth... And those eyes... they were the darkest green in the soft light of the street lamps.

"Hey," Madison managed to mumble. "What are you doing here?"

"I just came from the park," he said, catching up with her. "There's a basketball court there, so we go play sometimes. Didn't expect it to last this long, but we ended up with a tie and had to do a re-match."

"Did you win?" Madison asked with a smirk.

"Of course." Scott winked. "Want to walk home together? Your house is on the way to mine."

Did she want to walk home with Scott? *Yes, please.*

"What are *you* doing out so late?" he asked, and gave her a subtle once-over that made shivers spider-walk from her heels up the back of her legs and all the way up her spine to her nape. "Not playing basketball, I guess," he joked.

"Book club night." Madison smiled shyly as she started walking. "The discussion got a bit more heated than anticipated and we finished late…"

"Oh, which book?"

"*Northanger Abbey.* We're reading the classic version alongside a modern retelling that stirred a literary fire."

"The retelling, is it any good?"

"Why? You enjoy reading Jane Austen?"

"Hey, I might be a dude, but we're not all like Mark Twain. I love Jane; I don't want to 'dig her up and beat her over the skull with her own shin bone' every time I read *Pride and Prejudice*."

"So have you read it many times?"

"Ah, it's a truth universally acknowledged that a book lover has to read it more than once."

Scott was walking her home, and now, on top of looking gorgeous in his sporty clothes, he was quoting Jane Austen at her. Could a guy get any more perfect? Madison bit her lower lip so forcefully she almost drew blood. How was she supposed to get over him? *But I need to… I have no choice. Scott doesn't want me, he'll never want me. He has Haley… why would he ever spare me a second glance?*

"So," Scott continued, "is *Pride and Prejudice* your favorite Austen novel?"

"Nah, I'm more of a *Persuasion* kind of girl. I identify better with Anne Elliot than Elizabeth Bennet."

Scott gave a slight double take. "Not searching for your Mr. Darcy, then?"

You are my Mr. Darcy.

STOP IT, her conscience raged inside her.

Madison cleared her throat to hide her internal battle. "It's not about the hero, but the leading lady. Lizzy is too fierce, and I'm not. And my family… they can be pushy, just like the Elliots."

"You mean they persuaded you to break off an engagement with the love of your life?"

Madison giggled. "No, it's more of a modern-day issue."

Scott raised his eyebrows interrogatively.

"My dad wants me to become a lawyer to join the family business," Madison explained.

"Ah, and you don't want to?"

"No, never have."

"What would you want to do?"

Madison stared up at the night sky, wondering

why she was pouring her heart out to Scott. She never discussed her plans and dreams for the future with anybody, so why open up to him? *You know why...* Yeah, she did. But what good could come of it?

"I'm sorry," Scott said. "You probably don't want to discuss your entire life plan on your way home on a random Monday night."

"No, it's not that." Madison turned to look at him and found his bright green eyes trained on her. It made her knees go soft. "It's just that when you ask someone what they want... I mean, I doubt there's a harder question to answer, right?"

"Touché."

"If I had to tell you my biggest dream, it'd be to be a writer. To live in a small, remote cottage on the beach on the coast of Maine. Somewhere cold, with a view of a lighthouse, and only the sound of waves as a companion."

"Sounds tempting..."

"You like to write, too?"

"Yeah, I love it."

"Fiction, poetry...?"

"A bit of both. You?"

"Mostly fiction... I like stories."

"So what's stopping you from following that dream?" Scott challenged.

"My father would never accept it. The only other Smithson who refused to be a lawyer is my cousin Ethan…"

"I'm sure they didn't burn him at the stake."

"No, but his father told him Harvard was no longer free for kids who didn't play the good little lawyer. So you see why I'm worried about becoming a penniless writer with so much debt on my shoulders. I would have to find a more reliable source of income. A job I could actually stomach that still had to do with books…"

"Like?"

"Like becoming a teacher, or working at a publishing house, or even a publishing startup."

"Seems like a good plan."

"More brave than good. I'm not sure I'll ever find the guts."

"Would you rather do a job you hate to make your dad happy?"

"No, I'm just saying that whatever I do, someone is going to be disappointed, and it won't be easy either way."

"No," Scott agreed. "Nothing worthwhile ever is."

Did that apply also to love? Madison wondered, and then she shifted the focus of the conversation away from herself. "Have you always wanted to be a doctor?"

Scott smiled. "So Haley has been talking about me?"

"She has."

I also might've had this little stalking habit of knowing everything about you even before you met her. But let's ignore the details, shall we?

"Anyway, being a doctor has always been the dream for me. A real stethoscope was my favorite toy as a kid; I never considered anything else…"

"What kind of doctor do you want to be?"

"Neurosurgeon."

Madison tried hard not be impressed. "Why?"

"The brain is the most fascinating organ in the entire human body; it can do the most extraordinary things…"

Or turn perfectly normal human beings into silly, lovesick girls who'd give up everything for a kiss from the boy they loved. *No, bad Madison. Scott is Haley's boyfriend… and even if he weren't, he'd never be interested in you.*

"I bet your parents are happy about you becoming a neurosurgeon," Madison said.

Scott's lips parted in a foxy grin. "They're not too cross about it, but the academic is going to be challenging enough for me."

"I'll take your word for it, science books are the only kind I avoid. Oh…" Madison stopped abruptly; she'd almost walked right past her building. She was so comfortable talking with Scott she hadn't been paying attention to the road. "We're here. Thanks for walking me home."

"No problem." Scott smiled again. "You think

Haley is still up?"

Oh. *Oh.* So that was why he'd walked her home. Scott wanted to catch Haley before she went to bed, probably only to give her the most romantic goodnight kiss and then go home.

"She was when I left earlier, can't say for now. You want to come up and check?"

Yeah, Madison, invite him up to see a girl who's not you. Smart move.

Why was she torturing herself like this? Was she really so desperate to spend five more minutes with Scott that she'd even put up with seeing him with Haley?

Yep!

For Madison, loving Scott from afar, spending time with him was like poking a wound or scratching away a dried scab. Nothing good could ever come out of it, but she couldn't control the impulse.

"I should probably text her." Scott unlocked his phone's screen. "It's pretty late."

He typed a quick text and they both waited to see if Haley would reply.

"She must be already in bed," Scott said after a while. "I'll catch up with her tomorrow."

Madison was about to insist for him to come up when she remembered the whole "Haley kissing David at the masquerade" drama. Maybe her best friend wasn't ready to see her boyfriend and have "the awkward talk" with him.

"Yeah, right. Now that I think about it, she mentioned she was having an early night," Madison said. "This is goodnight, then."

"Night."

Scott pulled her into a quick goodbye hug, turned on his heel, and jogged away into the night. Madison stood there at the bottom of the steps of her building, dumbfounded. Her skin burned in all the spots where it had just connected with Scott's. Her nostrils filled with his scent of clean soap mixed with a sheen of light sweat, probably from the game. And her eyes trained on the tall figure quickly disappearing into the darkness.

Haley

Haley stared at Scott's text, aghast. Fear paralyzed her even if the message only said:

Hey... you still up?

She gaped at the simple line of text while keeping her phone on the lock screen. If she didn't open the text, he wouldn't know she'd read it, meaning he'd think she was asleep, meaning she wouldn't have to reply or, *worse*, talk to him. Via text or in person, it didn't matter. Haley was so utterly terrified of the next time she'd have to talk to her boyfriend that her first irrational instinct was to postpone the moment. Even if she knew she was only making things worse.

The entrance door opened and then clicked shut, signaling that Madison had gotten home. Haley and Alice had said goodnight a while ago, but Haley was still wide awake. She was in bed, staring at the ceiling and trying to draft an I've-kissed-your-brother-but-it's-not-a-big-deal speech in her head.

Long, gut-wrenching conversations weren't her thing; she was more about short, direct communication. But how else could she explain to Scott all the layers of her feelings? Make him understand how much she loved him… and how little she cared about his brother.

Maybe it didn't have to be so complicated. How about starting with a simple goodnight text? Haley unlocked the screen and typed:

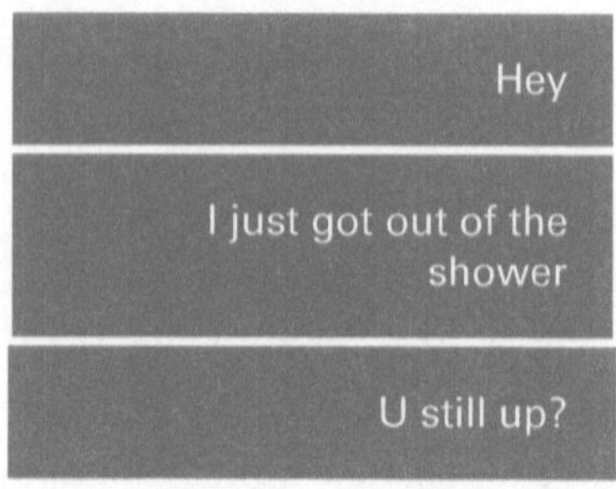

Walking into my room
right now

I need a shower, too

How was the game?

We won :)

Uh-huh

#TeamScott

Haley paused, undecided on what to type next. She *was* #TeamScott. Every cell in her body wanted him. David didn't matter, he'd been a summer fantasy almost a year ago and a real-life jerk for the past six months. He was mean and cruel, and this was only his latest stunt to try to ruin his brother's life. Haley wouldn't let him. She needed to make Scott understand. Her phone beeped again.

I was just outside your
building

Haley's heart contracted with a little pang.

She had nothing to worry about. Scott loved her, and he would believe her.

***

Haley wasn't feeling nearly so confident the next morning when she had to decide how and when to face her boyfriend. She used every possible excuse not to talk to him, in person or over the phone. Texts were okay for now. Haley had convinced herself that since she couldn't break the news with a text, it was perfectly normal not to mention the kiss in them. It wasn't like lying by omission.

She avoided him all of Tuesday, and on Wednesday morning, as she read Scott's early morning texts, she was ashamed to feel so completely relieved he'd be too busy to see her until later tonight. He had sent her a good morning kiss followed by a string of cute complaints:

Morning

:*

I'm so over the emojis

The real thing is so much better

Seems like forever I
haven't seen you

And today I'm busy all
day

I won't be home until later
tonight

Going downtown to
interview at
Massachusetts General
Hospital

For a different pre-med
program

They're going to give me
the tour of the hospital
afterward

So it'll take a while

Enough to give Haley a few more hours to prepare for her confession. But she couldn't postpone it any longer. Tonight, she must tell him.

Haley picked up her phone and hit reply.

I miss you too

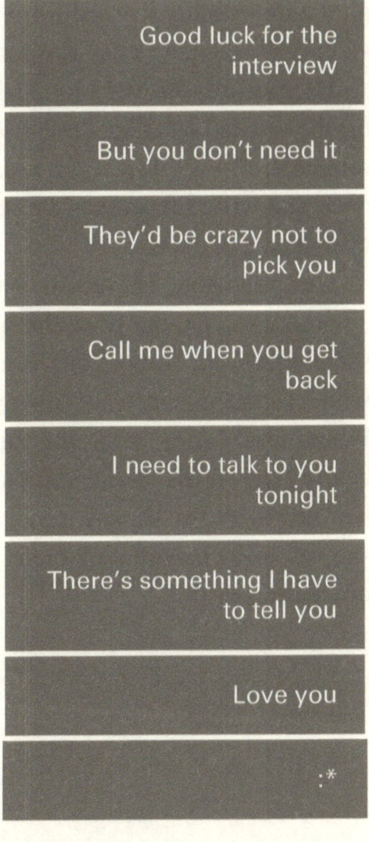

Haley had roughly eight hours to prepare herself. She should draft a speech and perhaps rehearse it on Alice. In normal circumstances, she would've asked Madison for help, since she was the best of the three of them with words, but she couldn't ask her friend to play Cyrano de Bergerac for her and Scott. Haley complimented herself on the literary quotation—totally learned from the Steve Martin and Daryl Hannah movie *Roxanne*.

Help or not, she had a job to do. Haley jumped off the bed and sat at her desk. Feeling particularly romantic, she decided to leave her laptop off for once and write the speech the old fashioned way using pen and paper.

Her decision proved a bad one for the environment. By the time she had a speech that satisfied her, the floor of her bedroom was littered with crumpled sheets of discarded drafts. But Haley was happy with the final result. After hearing her words, Scott wouldn't be able to turn her down. Now all she needed to do was to shower, make herself look pretty, and wait for her boyfriend to call.

Nine

Scott

On Wednesday night, Scott walked into his apartment lost in thought. The visit at Massachusetts General Hospital had gone well, and he was optimistic they'd accept him. So why did the thought make him so gloomy? Unconvinced, he peeked at the brochure still clutched in his hands. What was he complaining about? Massachusetts General was a top-tier hospital, and Dr. Salinger—Scott's would-be assigned doctor—was an excellent neurosurgeon.

But not the best.

Okay, not the best, but close. And this internship would be here in Boston, where he could stay with Haley all summer instead of them spending it three thousand miles apart.

Right.

He would get another chance to work with Dr. Allen. Sure, because opportunities like that just happened to rain on pre-med students, especially after they'd turned down medicine luminaries once already. Dr. Allen would simply sit there and wait for the wonderful Scott Williams to be his shadow whenever he chose.

Who am I kidding?

Students all over the U.S. would kill to get picked for that job, to be part—even if only as an observer—of Dr. Allen's research project. And the doctor had picked him, Scott. And he was about to turn down the offer, for a girl. But he'd do anything for her.

"Hello, brother." David's voice made him jump. Scott hadn't seen him half-hidden behind the kitchen bar. "Sorry, I didn't save you any dinner."

"Get lost, David."

A rundown with David was the last thing Scott needed right now.

"That's the best you can do? Ladies and gentlemen, please welcome on stage Scott Williams…" David banged a fork against a glass a couple of times and then dropped both into the dishwasher.

Scott refused to take the bait.

"No speech?" David continued. "I'll admit I was expecting more of a powerful opening."

"I said get lost."

"Oh, come on," David said, coming into the living room. "What's it gonna be?" He crouched slightly, hopping from one foot to the other and bringing his fists in front of his face in a defensive stance. The movements of a boxer in the ring. "Hook to the face?" David swung his elbow up and punched the air. "Sucker punch to the stomach?" He threw a low punch with his other hand. Then he straightened up—the boxing demonstration apparently over. "Personally, I'd prefer a raging shouting match. I would hate for us to get physical again. No one around to save your skinny ass this time."

Scott frowned. What the hell was David talking about?

"Wait, wait. Oooooh…" David's sneer widened. "You don't know…"

"Know what?"

Scott hated being at a disadvantage with David, and it looked like he was right now. David knew something that Scott didn't. Something that made David happy and that would, presumably, make Scott feel just the opposite. So much so that his brother had expected Scott to attack him as soon as he'd laid eyes on him. What was it?

"She hasn't told you…"

She. David meant Haley, Scott had no doubts now. His blood ran cold through his veins, and he rolled his fingers into tight fists, crushing the hospital brochure he was still holding.

"Told me *what?*"

"Oh." David shrugged and waved him off. "I wouldn't want to meddle."

Scott moved in a blur—in two quick strides he was on his brother. He grabbed David by the collar of his T-shirt and pinned him against the wall. They were almost nose to nose. "What did you do?" he hissed.

"I kissed her, brother." David spat the words in his face. "It was long and passionate. And she enjoyed every second of it."

Scott let go of his brother and staggered backward. He felt like he'd been hit multiple times in short sequence. Only David had used words instead of fists. "You didn't."

"Ask her if you don't believe me." David straightened the collar of his T-shirt. "We were reminiscing about it just the other night. Now, if you'll excuse me." David grabbed his phone and put it in his jeans pocket. "I had plans for tonight." He put on his black leather jacket and, with one last sly smile, he left.

Scott reeled backward until he hit the couch. David was a bastard and an asshole, but he wasn't a liar. He'd never said he'd kissed Haley if it wasn't true.

When had it happened? Was that why Haley had been kind of off lately? Scott had had the impression she'd been dodging him in the last couple of days… and now he'd found out why: she didn't want to confess.

No! The Haley he knew, the Haley he loved, would never cheat on him, especially not with David. She hated his brother. At least, that was what she'd always told him.

But David is no liar.

Scott's world tilted. He grabbed the couch backrest for support as angry tears streamed down his cheeks. In a blind rage, he punched the cushions in hard, fast strokes until his hand began to hurt. Taking deep breaths to try to calm himself, Scott took out his phone. He opened the messenger chat with Haley and scrolled through the past few days' conversations. Nothing in her texts pointed to a betrayal; they were full of sweet words, cute emoji, and I love yous.

But David is no liar.

He shuffled the chat to the end, his eyes resting on the last string of texts from her.

Call me when you get
back

I need to talk to you
tonight

There's something I have
to tell you

Love you

:*

Was "there's something I have to tell you" code for "tonight I'll admit I've cheated on you and dump your ass to be with your brother"? Could Haley really like David? Kiss him? It seemed so impossible…

But David is no liar.

Why else would she have kissed him?

Scott was still looking at the chat, searching for clues, when an email flashed into his inbox and invaded the top half of the screen. It was from Dr. Allen's office in California, reminding him they were still waiting for an answer from him about the shadowing program.

He loved Haley so much, and the last thing he wanted was to spend the summer away from her. But was he being stupid and naïve to give up an opportunity like this for a girl? Until an hour ago, Scott would've been sure the answer was no. He could already picture himself marrying Haley, one day after they were done with college and both had a job. He was devoted to her, and her to him. She wouldn't cheat on him, she just wouldn't…

But David is no liar.

The notion was like a drill into Scott's brain, and after hearing it so many times in his head, he started to believe it.

Jaw clenched, Scott wiped the tears from his cheeks with the back of his hand. He opened the email and, after reading the complete message, he tapped an impulsive reply…

Haley

Seven, and still no call. Haley was losing her mind. For the past hour, she'd been sitting at the dining table in her apartment staring at the black screen of her phone. She'd done all she could to postpone seeing Scott, but she'd spent the afternoon wishing time would fly faster… now that she had her speech ready, all this waiting was getting to her. And Scott should've been home by now.

"That phone will disintegrate in your hands if you grip it any harder," Alice said, staring at her dubiously. "I'm trying to make dinner here, but your anxiety is ruining my cooking chakra."

"Sorry," Haley said, releasing the hold a little. "I'm waiting for Scott to call. We're having the big talk tonight."

The book Madison was reading tumbled to the floor as she straightened abruptly. "You still haven't told him? Why?"

Haley shrugged and grimaced guiltily. "I've been busy, and so has Scott. I'm telling him tonight."

"Haley!" Madison pressed her palms to her

cheeks, shocked. "But he lives with *David*. What if the jerk tells him first?"

A sense of unease sneaked around Haley, tightening around her chest like an invisible rope. "David's never home, and he wouldn't."

"Um, hello?" Madison was getting all worked up. "Are we talking about the same person? Because the David I know wouldn't miss an opportunity like that to make people miserable. Especially his brother."

The unease worsened. Haley looked up at Alice chopping vegetables behind the kitchen bar for reassurance, but judging from her friend's worried expression, Alice seemed more aligned with Madison's line of thinking.

"Why don't you call him?" Alice said. "Instead of torturing yourself waiting."

"Okay."

With a pounding heart, Haley unlocked the screen and dialed Scott's number…

"It went to voicemail," Haley said, staring aghast at her friends.

Madison frowned and Alice stopped chopping her veggies.

"What do you think it means?" Haley asked.

"He could have forgotten to charge his phone?" Alice said tentatively.

Madison kept quiet; she just chewed her bottom lip like she did whenever she was nervous.

"Oh, no. No, no, nooo. If David got to him before I could explain… no!" Haley panicked. "I have to call him. Madison, do you have his number?"

"Scott's? No, why?"

"Not Scott's, David's…"

"Ah." Madison blushed. "Yeah, sure. I'm sending you the contact."

> **Maddie sent you a contact**
>
> **David**

Haley saved the number and pressed call.

He picked up on the third ring. "David's phone." There was music in the background and David sounded surprised, probably because he didn't recognize her number.

"Did you tell Scott?" Haley asked without preamble.

"I think I recognize that lovely tone of voice." The background music dimmed. Wherever he was, David must've moved to a quieter spot. "Nighty-night, Sunshine. What can I do for you?"

"Did you tell him?" Haley repeated.

"Tell him what?"

"David," she warned him. "I'm not in the mood for your games."

"Okay, fine. My brother and I had a heart to heart earlier."

"What did you say to him?"

"You sound worried… I only told the truth."

"What truth?"

"That we kissed, and that you enjoyed it… if memory serves me well."

Haley lowered the phone and closed her eyes, holding back the tears that were already threatening to spill.

After a few steadying breaths, she lifted the phone back to her ear, saying, "You know that's not the truth."

"No? Where's the lie?"

"Did you make it sound as if I cheated on him?"

"I stuck to the facts. No more. No less."

"So did you tell him the kiss happened before I even met him?"

"Um, that detail could've slipped my mind."

"You bastard."

"Ah, but I seem to remember that half-truths like I'm-not-lying-but-I'm-not-telling-you-everything made you tick."

"What are you talking about?"

"It worked pretty well for Scott when he told you how I was mad at him because a girl in high school chose him over me, forgetting to say I was *with* that girl when he started screwing her behind my back."

"I don't have time for this." Haley hung up. "You were right," she told Madison. "David is an asshole and I'm an idiot for leaving him the space to work his stupid tricks." It was adrenaline alone that kept Haley from collapsing in tears. "What do I do now?"

"Go find Scott," Alice said.

"You need to explain everything to him," Madison added. "It will be fine, he loves you."

"Go," Alice repeated. "Don't waste another second."

Haley jumped up, grabbed her bag, and dashed out of the house at a run.

Ten

Madison

"You think she'll make it?" Alice asked.

"Scott lives only a few blocks away, she'll get there in time," Madison said. "From the sound of that call, David must have just told Scott. There's nothing Scott could have done in the last few hours that Haley can't fix."

"Yeah, you're right. Scott doesn't seem like an impulsive guy. He wouldn't just head out and hook up with a random girl for revenge."

"No, never." Madison shook her head. "That's not him."

"Did you have dinner?"

"Not yet."

"Want some salad?" Alice offered. "I made extra."

"Sure."

Madison watched Alice set the table for two and plate the salad. They sat and started eating together.

"Mmm," Madison mumbled after the first forkful. "This is delicious, what's your secret?"

"Balsamic vinegar glaze."

"Awesome."

"So…" Alice paused. "Besides having an amazing cook for a roommate… how's everything else going? We didn't really get to talk after the… ah… wedding."

"Yeah, sorry for bailing on you and making you go home with Ethan and Rose, that must've been awkward."

"Your cousin was a bit grumpy, but now I understand why. And his girlfriend… Well, Rose is too damn nice to dislike, even for me. Plus, I found a nice surprise when I got home." Alice couldn't help smiling a little. "So I can't complain."

"Yeah, your surprise tried to talk to me, but I blew him off." Madison paused to swallow. "I'm so happy you guys are finally together, you deserve to be happy after waiting for so long."

"Maddie, it's only been a few days." Alice dropped her fork and stared into space. "But it's like everything I imagined, only ten times better."

Alice's smile was so radiant, and Madison tried to match its warmth, but how could she when her chest had transformed into a huge empty box with nothing in it?

Alice must've noticed, because she said, "Haley told me David has not been very *gracious* about your breakup."

Madison scoffed. "What else could I expect? You warned me about him, everyone did, but I didn't want to listen. I don't know, David seemed like a perfect distraction. And the breakup didn't hurt so much because I didn't care about him. I honestly wasn't that into him. He was a pretty face and great sex—don't tell Haley…"

"No way." Alice's eyes widened. "Our roommate is already confused enough."

"Anyway, it wasn't *because* we broke up that it got to me, it was *how* it happened. When David gets mad, he's scary and mean… I've never had a guy yell at me like that… And now I'm just glad it's over."

"And what about Scott?" Madison was about to deny everything as usual, but Alice anticipated her. "And please don't say you haven't got feelings for him," Alice added, "because we both know that's not true. I get why you don't want to talk with Haley about it, but I'm here. You can trust me, and you need to open up to someone about it. So, out with it."

Madison pushed her empty plate away and after flattening her palms on the table, she rested her forehead on the back of her hands. "Am I that obvious?"

"Only to me." Alice squeezed her arm. "Is it getting any better? It's been a few months now…"

Madison stood back up, shaking her head. "In a way, it's getting worse."

"How?"

"Before, Scott was this cute guy in my class I admired from afar. But since he's been going out with Haley, I got, you know, to meet him. He started talking to me. When we have a class together, he stops to say hello or sits near me. The other night I bumped into him when he was coming back from a basketball game—"

"Yeah," Alice said. "Jack was out playing too."

"Anyway, Scott walked me home." Alice raised an eyebrow. "Only because he wanted to see if Haley was still up," Madison justified herself. "And we talked about books and what we like to write. Oh, Alice, knowing Scott makes it so much worse. I want nothing more than for all these stupid feelings to melt away. I don't want to like him. I don't want to feel this way about him. But I can't control it, it won't just go away. No matter how wrong it is."

"It'd be wrong only if you tried to steal him from Haley. This way it only sucks. And I know exactly how you feel; I spent the last three years of my life with that same exact feeling…"

"Yeah, but you got the guy in the end. I can't even hope for that because it'd mean Haley is heartbroken. I just don't know what to do."

"Listen, Maddie." Alice took her hands in hers. "Who knows if Scott and Haley will stay together, or if you'll ever get to be with him, or even want him anymore? You could meet someone who sweeps you off your feet tomorrow… And our lives are going to be so completely different in a year when we graduate, anyway. You just have to be strong and pull through. And whenever you feel like banging your head against the wall, or when you feel the impulse to do something crazy and stupid like, I don't know, kiss the groom at someone else's wedding…" Alice gave her a little squeeze that let her know it was okay, that she understood what had brought Madison to that extremely bad choice. "You come to me instead. Madison, you've always been there for me when I was down for Jack. I know I've been distant lately, but that's only because I'm an idiot. I got mad and petty, and I'm sorry…"

Madison's eyes prickled with tears. This was the first real conversation she'd had with Alice after the Jack fight. Their friendship hadn't felt the same since then—at least, not until today. And now Alice's warm smile told her things were finally back to how they were before—minus the weight of untold secrets looming over their heads.

"No, it's all my fault," Madison said, tears rolling down her cheeks. "I closed up in a ball of misery and left everyone who cares about me out. But I love you, and I missed our friendship so much."

Alice, too, was sniffling a little. "I know, I love

you too. Together we can get past anything."

"Thank you," Madison whispered. "I don't know where I'd be without you."

They hugged and shared a good old cry, just like best friends do.

Haley

"Scott, open the door." Haley pounded her fist on it again. She'd been trying to convince Scott to let her in for five good minutes now. She was hammering the door with one hand and compulsively pushing the doorbell with the other. "Scott, I know you're in there. Open up. Please, I need to explain to you. It's not what you think."

"How is it, then?" his strangled voice came from inside.

Haley stopped the attack on the door. "Please let me in." She rested both her hands and her forehead on the cold surface, imagining Scott on the other side doing the same.

A few long seconds stretched out before the lock clicked. Gingerly, Haley pushed the door open and stepped into the apartment. Scott was facing away from the entrance, presenting her with the sight of his broad shoulders. Haley closed the door behind her and stepped forward.

"Scott...?"

He turned, face red and blotched from crying, eyes bloodshot.

"Oh, Scott." She made to throw her arms around his neck, but he stepped away.

"Is it true?" he asked in an angry whisper.

"It's not what you think."

"Actually, it's very simple," Scott said in a glacial tone. Then he shouted, "Did you kiss him or not?"

"I did." Fresh pain registered on Scott's face, making Haley's heart crack. "But I didn't know who he was, or that he was your brother. I hadn't even met you yet."

Confusion now marked Scott's features. "What are you talking about?"

Haley dared to take another step forward; she grabbed Scott's wrists and dragged him toward the couch, where they both sat down. He seemed too shocked to protest. "Last summer," she explained. "I went to this masquerade ball upstate. It was one of those stupid parties where everyone has to wear a period costume and a mask—"

Scott yanked his wrists free. "Why are you telling me—?"

"Please let me finish," Haley interrupted. "Let me tell you the whole story, and then I can answer all your questions. Okay?"

He nodded.

"That night at the party, I met a guy. He was wearing a huge mask that covered most of his face. I danced with him, we took a walk in the park, and he kissed me."

"I don't need to hear about all the guys in your past."

"You need to hear about this one."

"Why?"

Haley sighed. "Because it was David."

The look of confusion on Scott's face intensified. "I don't understand."

"David and I met that night, we kissed, and that was it. Immediately after the kiss, the security staff came running after his friend because they were crashing the party. The guards chased the friend all the way through the garden to where we were standing. They ran away together, and I never saw his face or learned his name. I didn't recognize David in Hawaii, but I think he recognized me, and that's why he acted so aggressive from the start."

"You kissed him a year ago?"

"Yes."

"And you didn't know who he was?"

Haley shook her head.

Scott stood up and started pacing around scratching his head. "So this is all a twisted comedy of errors?"

Haley wasn't sure what a "comedy of errors"

entailed, and the situation couldn't be any less comic, but she nodded all the same.

Scott's features relaxed for a moment. Then his jaw tightened again. "How long have you known?"

"Only since Monday night. When I left here after seeing you, I forgot my phone. I came back to get it and David started acting all nasty as usual. We got into a fight, and that's when he told me."

"Is that why you've been avoiding me the past few days?"

"Yes," Haley admitted.

"Because you like him."

"No, Scott. I love *you*."

"Then why didn't you tell me?" He was near yelling again.

"Because I was afraid!" Haley shouted back, standing up from the couch.

Scott seemed taken aback by her sudden scream. "Of what?"

"That you would look at me differently, that you wouldn't want to be with me anymore…"

Scott shook his head. "He made it sound as if you'd cheated on me."

"I didn't." Haley took a step forward. "I would never do that to you. I've just been stupid, I should've told you right away… but I was so worried. I thought waiting a couple of days wouldn't be such a big deal. I should've known

David was going to be a dick about it. I'm sorry."

Scott sank back on the couch, dropping his head into his hands.

"Scott?" Haley sat next to him.

He looked up at her. "I wish you'd told me right away."

There was a haunted look in his green eyes that made Haley shiver. "Why?" she asked in a trembling voice.

"David never lies," Scott said. "When he said you two had kissed, I… I…"

"You what?"

"I believed him…"

There was something he wasn't telling her. "And?"

"I took the internship in California."

Haley breathed a sigh of relief. For a moment she'd imagined Scott going to town to make out with the first girl he saw. But the next second she wondered if Scott moving to the other side of the country was really any better.

"To punish me?" she asked.

"No. Yes. I don't know. I was blinded by rage and it sort of happened."

"How could it *sort of* happen?"

"I was looking at your texts from the past few days, trying to figure out what was happening, and they sent me a follow-up email. Without thinking, I replied that I was going."

"Because you wanted to get away from me."

"From you both." Scott lowered his head. "I thought you were going to leave me for him."

Haley took his face into her hands and lifted his chin. "Scott, look at me." He did. "I will never leave you for him. I love *you*. It will always be you."

Scott pressed his lips to hers. An urgent, passionate kiss that mirrored all of Haley's feelings. The way he pulled her close, the intensity of his need, was fueled like hers by the dread of losing each other, by the relief at it not being so, and by the longing already present for the time they would have to spend apart.

Scott lifted her bodily from the couch, and without ever breaking the kiss or saying another word, he brought her to his bedroom. They made love as if it was the first and last time, their bodies speaking to one another the way words never could…

Eleven

Haley

Haley stared at the moonlight filtering through the blinds, at the faint silver sheen it cast over Scott's room, making the silhouettes of his dresser, desk, and wardrobe barely distinguishable in the darkness. Scott was lying next to her on the bed, head resting on her chest as she stroked his hair.

"Can't you sleep?" he asked.

"No, sorry. Too many emotions today." Haley gave a soft chuckle. "I'm still pumped full of adrenaline."

Scott shifted positions and propped his head on an elbow as if to stare at her, even if in the darkness it was impossible. Haley could only distinguish the black contour of his straight nose. "Is adrenaline all that's keeping you awake?"

"Also guilt for not telling you about the kiss right away," Haley said. "And anger for leaving David room to come between us. I should've never done that." She sighed. "But Scott, after everything you told me about Brigitte, I would've hated for you to see me differently. For you to think I was the same as *that girl* from your past."

Scott cupped Haley's face with one hand.

"Hey, you're nothing like Brigitte. She was a liar and a schemer, a mean girl who enjoyed toying with people's lives. You only made an honest mistake. We both did. I, too, left David room to play his tricks. I should've trusted you. No matter what he claimed, I should've called you instead of taking his word for it and making life-changing decisions in the heat of the moment."

"Yeah." Haley wasn't able to keep a bittersweet note out of her voice. "I hadn't pinned you down as impulsive. You always seem so calm and reflective."

"I am impulsive when it comes to you." He tapped her nose with a finger in an affectionate gesture. "You make me literally lose my mind, usually in a good way. But today… when I thought I'd lost you… to him. I went off the wrong deep end."

Haley didn't say anything, so Scott asked, "Are you worried because we're going to spend the summer apart?"

Haley traced his profile with a finger. "I'm not thrilled you're going away for two months, but I'm happy you took the internship, honestly. It was too good an opportunity to pass up on, just for me. And I'm not worried about us, I trust you completely."

"And I trust you." Scott pulled her closer. "But the idea of spending so much time apart… I don't want to."

"Two months will fly by," Haley lied.

"Come with me," Scott breathed down her neck and started kissing her collarbone.

The sensation was so good, Haley was almost ready to throw all her other obligations out the window and say yes. But she couldn't.

Pulling back, she said, "I can't. Even if I wanted to, it's too late to get a refund on tuition, and I can't just throw all that money away."

"And I can't stay." Scott sounded heartbroken. "I already confirmed with Dr. Allen's staff, and I wrote to Massachusetts General to notify them I've accepted another offer."

"Gah, you've been thorough." Haley sniffled, trying not to burst into tears. "You must've really hated me."

"I could never hate you." Scott stamped a soft kiss on her lips.

"But you're going to California."

"Unless I want to spend the summer doing nothing, I have to."

Suddenly cold, Haley lifted the bedspread over her shoulders. "Where does that leave us?"

"In a long-distance relationship for two months?"

"You don't want to take a break?"

"No, never. Why would I want a break? I'm in love with you."

"So the fact that I kissed David doesn't change the way you feel about me?"

Scott stiffened next to her. "The thought of his lips"—he traced hers with a finger—"on this mouth makes me want to punch a wall. I'm jealous of my brother and he is jealous of me in a way it's hard to explain if you don't have a sibling… But the past doesn't change how much I love you, not for a second."

"Are you sure?"

Scott pushed a lock of hair away from her forehead. "After David told me about the kiss, I wanted to die, to disappear, to go as far away as possible… and now I'd give anything to take it all back, but I can't. I've always wanted to be a doctor and I need this internship. I've been so stupid to believe—"

"No, you haven't." Haley laced her fingers with his, bringing their joined hands to rest over her heart. "David never lies," she said. "It's something he knows you've always trusted, and he used it against you, but it's not your fault for believing him."

"I just keep wishing that I'd waited a few hours. Or I think about what would have happened if I hadn't seen the email. I'm torturing myself imagining everything else that could've stopped me from sending that damned response."

"And my brain is stuck in a loop of 'if only I'd

told him sooner.' But I didn't and you didn't and there's nothing we can do about it now. David twisted the truth and used it against us, but we can't let him win."

"He's already won, he got exactly what he wanted… to keep us apart."

"It doesn't matter where we are, physically. We're still going to be together. David hasn't won anything."

"It still sucks."

Haley scoffed. "Agreed."

She noticed that Scott wasn't asking any questions about the kiss. How it'd been. If Haley had enjoyed it. If she'd thought about David after that night. He had asked if she liked David while they were still in the middle of a shouting match, but nothing afterward. Maybe Scott didn't want to know. Or he could be afraid of what answers she might give him. And he'd be right, because the truth wouldn't make the kiss any easier to digest for him.

If he ever asks, I'm not going to lie, Haley promised herself, before shifting the topic to more practical aspects. "When does the internship start?"

"June 20th… It's a Monday, but I'll have to get to California a couple of days early to find a place to live and get settled."

"So you're basically leaving in a week."

"I haven't planned anything yet."

"And you won't have much time to plan," Haley said, straddling him. "Because I'm going to want to spend every minute you have left here together." She kissed him.

"Hey." Scott ran his hands down her lower back. "It's just a summer… nothing will change."

"You promise?"

"I promise."

Scott

Scott didn't bump into his brother again for the next two days. On Friday morning he found David seated at the kitchen bar wearing a suit and eating cereal out of a bowl as if he didn't have a concern in the world.

Scott stopped dead in the middle of the living room, undecided on what to do. A part of him wanted to scream at his brother, to beat him into a pulp. But at the same time, he wanted to pretend David didn't exist.

"Oh, come on, brother," David said. "No need for that disapproving scowl. I've heard the princess come and go these past few nights… Guess all is well again in paradise?"

"No thanks to you."

Scott had to muster all his self-control not to get dragged into another argument with David. Better to skip breakfast and leave before he did something he'd regret.

But his brother wasn't as ready to ignore him.

"May I ask why you stole the coffee maker?" David said, in a perfectly conversational tone. "Is caffeine deprivation your ultimate revenge strategy?"

"The coffee maker is mine and I can do whatever the hell I want with it."

"Are you finally moving out?" David asked. "Couldn't help but notice you're getting all boxed up. How are you going to afford a new place?"

"If you really have to know, I'm moving to California for the summer for an internship."

"Woooh." David smiled viciously. "I hope my little slip of the tongue had nothing to do with your sudden decision to move cross-country."

"What do you want me to say, David? That your mastermind plan to ruin my life worked? Well, bravo." Scott clapped his hands mockingly. "You're officially a dick."

David licked his spoon and dropped it into the bowl before saying, "At least now you've tried first-hand how fun half-truths can be."

"What are you talking about?"

David's blue eyes flared. "You know what."

"Not Brigitte again. How many times do I have

to tell you that I didn't know?"

"How convenient…"

"I can't do this again, you refuse to listen—"

"Oh, I hear you just fine. Pity I don't believe you." David got up from the stool and rounded the kitchen bar, his eyes searching Scott's face. "Were you really dumb enough not to notice? Not to ever wonder?"

Scott didn't reply.

"Come on, Scotty, say it," David pushed. "Let it out, you'll feel better afterward, I promise."

"I DIDN'T KNOW!" Scott shouted, exasperated.

"Didn't know?" David spoke in a quiet hiss, his cold fury topping Scott's blunt anger. He took a step forward and shoved Scott backward. "Or didn't *want* to know?"

David gave him another push until Scott's back was pressed against the wall. In a quick move, his brother jagged his forearm against Scott's throat, leaving him just enough room to breathe. "Tell me, brother," David said, still speaking in a soft, angry whisper. "Whenever Brigitte told you not to make your relationship public, to keep it a secret from me, you never suspected it might be because she was still *with* me? Never?" David pinned him with a glacial blue stare. "Not even once?"

Scott lowered his gaze, unable to sustain his

brother's glare. The truth was that, deep down, he had suspected something was wrong with the way Brigitte had behaved. Scott hadn't known for sure, but he had preferred to look the other way. To pretend he believed her version one hundred percent.

"There." David gave him another light shove and then let him go, bouncing backward. "Feels good to finally admit the truth, doesn't it?"

Scott wiped his mouth with the back of his hand. "What do you want me to say?"

"Apologize for once. Admit you didn't care if what you were doing was wrong, because you wanted Brigitte more than anything you'd ever wanted in your life. And even after you found out the truth, you still didn't care…"

"I am sorry, David. I've been sorry for a long time. But can't you see she strung both of us along? We both loved her, and she probably didn't care about either of us. Can't we just let that go? Start over?"

"Nice speech. One I could've respected if you hadn't decided to fish in my pond again."

"*Your* pond?" Scott scoffed. "Because you kissed a girl one night, a girl who couldn't even tell who you were?"

"It was a rather special kiss."

"I've been with Haley for the past six months, in case you haven't noticed. I never knew you'd met her first, and now it's too late to call dibs."

"Seriously? You didn't know? Is that your good-for-all excuse?"

"Haley is with me now. Forget the fantasy and open your eyes to reality."

"I want what I want, brother."

"Keep your hands off her," Scott threatened.

"That, brother, is only for Haley to decide."

"She hates you."

"Mmm… maybe…" David's mouth curled up at the corners, his eyes sparkling with malice. "Well, then, you have nothing to fear." He straightened his tie and jacket and opened the door. "I only hope she doesn't get too lonely while you're gone…" David waved mockingly. "Bon voyage."

Twelve

Haley

Scott's last week in Cambridge seemed to fly by for Haley in no time at all. Being both still free from any other commitment, they spent every minute available together—mostly in bed. But all too soon, the last day before the departure arrived.

Haley barged into her apartment, eager to grab a change of clothes and be back on her way toward Scott's house.

"Hey, you're alive," Alice joked from the kitchen. "I'm making coffee, want some?"

"Hi… no, thanks. I'm just going to pick up a few things and go back to Scott's place. It's our last night together."

"How're you holding up?

"Super-duper," Haley said sarcastically. "I'm kinda in a hurry… Mind if we talk another time? Tomorrow I can tell you all about how sad and depressed I really am."

"Yeah, about that." Alice stepped into the hall to face her. "I wanted to give you a heads-up…"

"About what?"

"Did you have anything special planned for tonight?"

"No, Scott and I are just going to hang out at his place. Why?"

"Good, because the guys are planning a send-off party, Jack told me about it."

Haley didn't think it possible, but her mood worsened dramatically. The last thing she wanted tonight was to *party*. Parties were for celebrations, and there was absolutely nothing to celebrate here. "A party?"

"More of a dinner, really. I told Jack to tone it down as much as he could."

"Can't you tell him to call it off entirely?" Haley hated the way she sounded super petty, and the fact that in the span of a week she'd become the neediest, clingiest girlfriend. But she couldn't help being selfish. Scott was leaving and every minute they weren't alone together felt like wasted time.

"Too late for that." Alice shrugged apologetically. "Jack left only a few minutes ago, but he was going to give Scott a call." Disappointment must've shown on Haley's face, because her roommate hastened to add, "But I'll ask him to book a table early and I'll make sure they keep it short. I'll also tell Jack and the others not to insist on going for drinks afterward. Sound good?"

Haley relaxed. Alice was only trying to help, and Scott's friends had a right to say bye to him before he left. As much as she hated it, Haley would have to share. "Yeah," she said, pulling Alice into a hug. "Sorry for being so snappish, I'm in an awful mood."

Alice patted her back supportively. "I know, babe."

Just as they pulled apart, the apartment door opened again.

"Hi, roomies," Madison said, coming in. "What's up?"

"I was telling Haley the boys are organizing a dinner for tonight to say goodbye to Scott."

"Aw." Madison unconsciously lowered her gaze to the floor for a second before staring back up at them. "Sounds fun."

"Can you make it?" Haley asked, to let Madison know she was invited.

"Mmm… yeah, I'm free tonight."

"Great. Can I also ask you a favor?"

"Sure. What do you need?"

Haley felt super shitty for what she was about to ask, but Madison was still one of her best friends. And they had an unspoken agreement not to let the fact that they both were in love with the same guy change their friendship. And if Scott were any other guy, Haley wouldn't have had a problem asking her best friend for a favor… so…

"Can I borrow your car tonight?" Haley asked. Madison was the only one out of the three of them with a car. Her entire family was from Boston and she'd literally just driven a few blocks from home to come to Harvard. "I want to give Scott a ride to the airport; I would hate it if he had to take an Uber."

"Yeah, of course." Madison smiled, her cheeks reddening. "Do we need to drive tonight?" she asked Alice.

"No, Jack wanted to keep it walking distance."

"Perfect." Madison grabbed the keys from the small cabinet in the entrance and handed them to Haley. "The tank's full, you should make it to Logan Airport and back without troubles."

"Thank you." Haley took the keys and hugged Madison. "You're the best."

"No problem."

"Well, I'd better get going." Haley put the keys in her bag so as not to forget them, then dashed for her room, saying, "I'll see you both later."

***

Less than an hour later, Haley was lounging on Scott's bed, back against the wall, MacBook open in her lap. She was keeping him company while he packed. And to distract herself from the reality of Scott's largest suitcase lying open on the floor, Haley was playing around with some data. The self-assigned task was to organize a large set of scattered figures into a statistical report that would make sense. Yeah, a geek at heart.

Haley was focused on a particularly dense section when Scott's voice penetrated her concentration. "I know you wanted to spend tonight alone, but Jack called—"

"Alice told me about the party," Haley interrupted. "No worries. You know who's going to be there?"

"Just you girls and a few of the guys on the team, the ones still around."

"Is David still MIA?" she asked.

"Yep," Scott said, folding a sweatshirt. "Haven't seen him or heard from him since our latest brotherly chat."

Haley abandoned her numbers for a second to watch Scott. "It's good that you finally discussed the Brigitte issue, though, isn't it? It's the first step to fix your relationship…"

"Brigitte isn't the issue between us anymore… you are."

"Then you have no issues at all because I'm with you and that's never going to change."

Scott squatted low, turning his back to her as he rearranged a few items inside his almost-full suitcase. "So that kiss really meant nothing to you?" he asked, almost casually. "Because David keeps hinting it was a big deal."

Ah, the dreaded question had finally arrived.

Haley squirmed on the bed. Alice's advice to play down the truth rang in her ears. But she'd promised to herself she wouldn't lie to Scott. "I was caught up in it at the time." She watched his shoulders tense. "But more in a fairy tale fantasy sort of way. It wasn't real… And, honestly, I hadn't thought about it in forever, because now I have you."

Scott got up, a slight grimace on his face. His expression said he didn't like what he was hearing, but he thanked her for the honesty.

"TMI?" Haley asked.

"No." Scott walked toward her. "You kissed David. I don't like it, but I'll have to deal with it." He leaned in to retrieve a stack of underwear from the chest of drawers near the bed, throwing a peek at her Mac's screen as he bent. "What are all those numbers?" Scott asked, as if nothing of importance had been said, the let's-change-the-subject subtitle all too clear.

"A baseline of data. I'm trying to build a sorting algorithm."

"My eyes cross just looking at it. I've always hated calculus and math."

"Maybe the theory, but once you see what you can do with all the formulas, it's amazing. Like, here, take this data—when it's raw and unprocessed, it's pure chaos… but when the algorithm sorts and organizes the numbers, they begin to tell a story."

Scott threw a skeptical glance at the sheet. "Sorry." He shrugged. "Still looks like gibberish. I prefer stories told in words. Numbers were never my thing."

Haley rolled her eyes, disappointed. Scott never shared her enthusiasm for computers and programming. And whenever he tried to enlighten her on the beauty of poetry, she often found herself half bored to death. The only novels Haley enjoyed reading were sci-fi sagas and the occasional vampire novel—books all too commercial for Scott's literary fiction tastes—and she preferred to watch the movie versions of most books anyway. Both Scott and Madison would gag if they heard her say this aloud.

She pressed save and shut her laptop; it was getting too warm on her legs, anyway. Haley threw a wistful glance at the brimming case on the floor. "Almost done here?" she asked, tearing her eyes away from the suitcase and its implied meaning. Scott was leaving her... Tomorrow, he'd be gone. *It's only two months,* she kept repeating to herself.

"Yeah, I need socks..." He took them out of another drawer and shot six balled pairs into the suitcase, basketball style—feet in a slightly staggered stance, body elongated, arms up, and six flicks of the wrist—sending all the tiny balls to land precisely in the center of the suitcase. He looked sexy as hell, like whenever he was on the basketball court. "…And I'm done."

He smiled, and Haley couldn't resist—she swung her legs off the bed and pulled him to her before he could go close the suitcase. She rested her hands on his hips, looking up at him. "So what's the latest housing plan?"

"I've booked a Holiday Inn for tomorrow and Friday night. And I have six housing appointments scheduled; I hope to find a place before the weekend."

"I liked the one near the beach."

Haley had helped him sort through the Craigslist listings to choose which appointments to book.

"Of course you liked that one." Scott dropped his hands on her shoulders, his thumbs caressing her trapezius muscles. "But it's also the farthest away from the hospital, and everyone says traffic sucks in California."

"It's not like you'll be driving."

"No, exactly. I hope the condo two blocks from work will be cool."

"The apartment-share with the residency student?"

"That one."

"Aren't residents supposed to be super busy and never at home?" Haley's hands sneaked under

Scott's tank top and up his lower back. "Don't you want to meet someone who'll introduce you to loads of people? You don't know anyone over there."

"I don't expect Dr. Allen to be a nine-to-five kind of guy; shadowing him will be worse than any residency. There won't be much time for me to get social."

"I wish I could believe you." Haley pouted jokingly. "You'll meet tons of blonde Californian beauties and forget all about me."

Scott gently pulled at the ends of her just-above-the-shoulders bob. "Pity I have a thing for brunettes…"

"You do, huh?"

"I do." Scott's smile disappeared, and he became suddenly serious. "I'm going to miss you," he said, dropping his forehead to hers.

"Me, too." Haley lifted her chin to kiss him.

In a blur of passion and longing, they tore each other's clothes off and rolled onto the bed, their limbs so entangled it was impossible to tell where one body started and the other ended…

Thirteen

Haley

"We're going to be late," Haley said, her mind still hazy from all the goodbye sex.

If nothing else, Scott's imminent departure had given her the best week of sex of her life. There was something to be said about making love knowing you were about to be separated from your partner for a long time. It heightened everything. Every kiss, every touch, every sensation was more urgent, intense, powerful…

Scott groaned, stretching beside her. "I don't care…"

"The sooner we leave," Haley grazed the skin of his neck with her teeth, "the sooner we can come back and do this again."

"I'm convinced." He flashed her a roguish smile and hopped off the bed.

They took a quick shower—*together*—and managed to get to the restaurant only ten minutes late. To their relief, they weren't even the last to arrive. Alice and Jack beat them to it and, judging from the healthy glow on both their faces, for the same reason.

Once they were all seated, Haley fought hard to keep a smile plastered on her face. But inside, she couldn't help the relentless countdown her brain had initiated. Her stupid mathematical mind enjoyed providing her with a set of depressing numerical stats Haley could've gladly done without. 12 hours until Scott's plane left. 720 minutes. 43,200 seconds. 72 days before he came back. 1,728 hours. 103,680 minutes. And a ridiculous number of seconds. Okay, now she could get Scott's hatred for numbers.

How was she supposed to endure all that time without him? It wasn't that Haley had never been single, or that she didn't know how to be on her own. But in the last six months, she'd relinquished most of that independence to her relationship. She'd gotten used to Scott's presence by her side. To always have his support, to see him almost every day, to make love to him whenever she wanted, and to always be able to count on him… And now she'd have to learn how to be alone all over again.

Besides disturbing numerical statistics and even gloomier thoughts, Haley was having a hard time deciding what she found more annoying about this farewell party. The way Madison kept trying—*and failing*—not to stare at Scott adoringly. How Alice seemed to pick up on everything and kept alternating worried side glances between Haley, Madison, and Scott. The frankly tasteless jokes the "boys" kept bouncing off Scott about Californian beauties. *Hello? His girlfriend is sitting right next to you, assholes.* Or the fact that every minute they spent at this restaurant was a minute less Haley could have Scott all for herself.

Usually the most social and outgoing in her group of friends, tonight Haley felt like a bratty child who hadn't gotten what she'd wanted for Christmas. While her family was all happy and busy celebrating, she was left alone sulking in a corner—ignored.

Get a grip, *she told herself.* You're ruining this for Scott, stop being a total bitch.

Haley took a deep breath and got up to go to the restroom. A splash of fresh water on her face and she'd be as good as new and back to being a decent human being and not a sorry girlfriendzilla.

She'd barely made it to the hall leading to the restrooms when someone grabbed her from behind.

"I know you'd rather be back home," Scott breathed down her neck. "Me, too."

Goosebumps traveled all the way down from Haley's nape to the tip of her toes.

"Busted?" she asked, turning around.

Scott nodded, opening his arms invitingly.

Haley burrowed her face in his chest. "I'm sorry, it's your goodbye party and I'm ruining it for you. But I can't help being in an awful mood."

"Hey." Scott made her look up. "You're not ruining anything. I know every minute we spend here seems like a minute less we can be together, but I promise I'll make it up to you."

Scott had a wicked twinkle in his eyes and Haley couldn't help but smile and ask, "Make up for it, huh? How?"

Scott whispered the mischievous answer in her ear and made to lead her back to the others before she could reply.

"Hey," Haley protested, "what if I really needed the restroom?"

Scott flashed her a grin. "Did you?"

"No," Haley admitted, and let him pull her away.

Back at the table, they spent the rest of the evening eye-flirting with each other. The entire dinner didn't seem wasted time anymore, just a long session of hands-off foreplay. Haley couldn't stop smiling—for real this time. Never in her life had she had this much complicity with anyone. Not a guy. Not her friends. Only Scott. It would always be Scott.

***

Hours later, in Scott's room, Haley was staring at the dark ceiling, a whirlwind of sad thoughts swirling ceaselessly inside her head. After a night together that needed to last them two months, they were both spent and could not have made love another time even if they'd wanted to.

"You're not sleeping," Scott said, turning on the bed to face her.

"Neither are you."

"I can't sleep with you so awake next to me."

Haley huffed the hair away from her face. "Sorry, but I don't want to sleep."

"Why not?"

"Because you're here now and sleep is a waste of time." Haley sighed. "I can sleep tomorrow all day if I want to. Hell, I can sleep every day for the next two months... but not tonight, not while you're still with me."

"Night... it's almost dawn already."

"Wilt thou be gone?" Haley whispered. "It is not yet near day."

Scott propped himself on an elbow, surveying her. "Are you quoting Shakespeare at me?" he asked with a grin barely visible in the faint light that preceded dawn. "I thought you hated verses and plays and poetry..."

"I do." Haley smirked.

Scott frowned in the semi-darkness.

"End of the nineties," she announced in a dramatic voice, "Leonardo DiCaprio and Claire Danes co-star in the most epic movie of the decade…"

Scott groaned. "*That* movie, seriously?"

"Hm-mmm," Haley hummed. "*Romeo + Juliet* was one of my favorite movies growing up. I learned it almost by heart."

"You liked the movie, or Leonardo DiCaprio?"

"Bit of both."

Haley smiled, and Scott tickled her sides. The game soon ended in a kiss, and when Scott pulled away, he didn't move back to his side of the bed. He knelt half on top of her, caressing her hair.

"I appreciate the literary quote," he said. "But we're nothing like Romeo and Juliet."

"No? Feels a lot like it."

"What? Like we're star-crossed lovers who just got married in secret because our families are mortal enemies and now I've killed your cousin and I'm being exiled?" Scott taunted.

"No," Haley said, her tone serious. "Like you have to leave and I don't want you to."

"I have more care to stay than will to go," Scott recited theatrically. "I'll stay and lose my flight… Haley wills it so."

"No, she doesn't. Haley wills you to go do your wonderful internship and learn everything you can from your superstar doctor. But she wants you to stay at the same time… if it makes any sense?"

"Completely, because I want to go and to stay just as much."

As if on cue, Scott's phone lit up, and the alarm started beeping.

"But you have to go," Haley said.

Scott gave her a peck on the lips and sat on the bed to silence the phone. Haley knelt behind him, hugging his back.

She leaned in and bit his earlobe. "Think we have time for one last bit of fun before your exile?"

Scott didn't have to be told twice. "My snooze time is pretty long." He dropped the phone and turned, pinning Haley on the bed underneath him. Turned out they still had some steam in them.

***

The drive to the airport was a sad business spent mostly in silence. Haley was busy driving Madison's car and getting too much inside her own head, and Scott was evidently exhausted after a sleepless night. Haley knew him well enough to see he was already focused on all the things he needed to sort out before Monday.

After a quick breakfast outside of the security check barrier, the time to really say goodbye came. Tears already welling in her eyes, Haley followed Scott toward the gate as far as non-passengers were allowed. She kept her gaze trained on the floor the entire time to hide her puffy red eyes, and when they stopped, Scott had to lift her chin to make her look at him.

"Please don't cry," he whispered, pulling her into a hug.

Haley inhaled his familiar scent, and that did it—the last shred of self-control she'd hung to slipped away, and she started sobbing uncontrollably.

"It's okay," Scott said, caressing her hair. "I'll be back in no time."

"I know, I'm just being silly."

"No, you're not." Scott pulled back slightly and cupped her face in his hands. "I love you."

"I love you."

He kissed her one last time—okay, more three or four kisses all rolled into one heart-wrenching goodbye—and then he walked away.

Haley watched him go through security until Scott was on the other side. He turned to flash her a sad-ish grin while he raised the hand holding the plane ticket in a final farewell gesture. And then he was gone.

The moment Scott disappeared behind the corner, a cold, heavy stone replaced Haley's heart.

Be fickle, Fortune, *Haley thought, feeling just as ill-divining as Claire Danes in the movie,* for then I hope thou wilt not keep him long. But send him back.

Back to me, and fast... Haley took the poetic license of adding.

Fourteen

Haley

Scott was gone, and the only thing that made Haley get out of bed on Monday morning was the start of summer classes. After a weekend spent holed up in her room watching *Romeo + Juliet* on repeat, Haley was glad something was forcing her to react. With two grad computer science courses and an advanced statistics class on her plate, she hoped she'd be too busy to mope over Scott.

He'd called every day since he'd gotten to California, but talking over the phone was a poor replica of a real-life conversation, and every single time he'd been in a hurry. Too many things to set up, too many places he needed to be. And he hadn't even started working yet. If things kept going this way, she'd be lucky if they managed to talk for more than ten minutes at a time.

Unfortunately, the first week of school proved all her fears right. The classes were demanding, but not nearly challenging enough to absorb Haley completely. She still had plenty of time to feel lonely. After almost seven months dating Scott, she was used to being held, kissed, and cuddled. The lack of physical contact was taking its toll, and the difficulties in talking to each other were rattling her emotionally. Conversations with Scott were officially counted in minutes—single digits—and not hours.

Saturday morning, still in this state of mind, Haley was positively scared of spending another full weekend in her room. She worried she'd end up with another forty-eight-hour marathon of tragic love movies and endless tears... so she decided to go to the library to do her homework. Usually, she didn't care to use a shared space to study. Library goers had a tendency of rolling their eyes at her constant keyboard click-clacking that made Haley uncomfortable. But staying home wasn't an option today. In a public location, Haley would have to get her act together, concentrate on her assignments, and she definitely wouldn't be able to watch any movie or cry.

Of all the facilities available on campus, Haley settled on the Widener Library. If she really had to go study somewhere, she might as well pick Harvard's flagship library. The building was an impressive brick rectangle, its front lined with huge white pillars that stood at the head of a flight of steps. Inside, the larger study room, Widener Loker Reading Room, had an old-style feel and was even more impressive with its high-vaulted light-green ceiling that let in plenty of natural light.

The place must've been a lot emptier than during a regular term, but still, all the long rectangular tables had two to three students already seated at them. Haley shuffled to the back of the room, toward a table with only two busy seats at the opposite ends. On the left, facing Haley, was an Asian girl in a red cotton sweater with long dark locks, her neck bent over a set of open tomes. On the right, there was an empty chair with a messenger bag strapped across its back and a laptop opened on an Excel sheet.

Haley's first instinct would've been to grab a seat in the middle, but the Excel sheet had caught her attention. Whoever was working on that model was doing a really poor job. To be fair, Haley could understand the base logic they'd applied. But they were going at it all wrong… a few lines of well-thought code inside an Excel macro could solve the problem in a matter of minutes. Otherwise, it'd take them hours…

Careful not to make it scrape, Haley drew back the second to nearest chair to the abandoned laptop and sat down, setting up her MacBook on the table. Where to start? The STAT S-106 homework assignment seemed to be calling to her. And while she worked at it, the fella next door could get a better idea of how data should be handled. Secretly, Haley hoped that whoever was going to sit next to her would realize how good of a job she was doing and plead for her help. She couldn't help it. When it came to numbers, she was such a show-off.

Shuffling the syllabus out of the way, Haley found the paper with the first homework assignment. Question one looked easy, a straight statistical analysis of a given pool of data, complete with Mean Absorbance Ratio, and prevalence calculations. Question number two, instead, was the open-ended kind Haley hated:

```
The Boston Mayor is determined to
assess the population satisfaction
with the performance of the Police
Department (PD) and the District
Attorney (DA) office in all the
city's counties.
You are in charge of the team
contracted to do the study and must
report to the Mayor.
- Who should you poll? Do you
attempt a census or opt for a well-
designed controlled poll/survey?
- What sample size(s) would you use?
What criteria do you need to satisfy
to argue about the validity of your
final conclusions?
```

The assignment continued with more stupid open questions. Ugh, what a waste of brainpower… going over the methodologies to acquire the data was so boring. Essential for any analysis to ever make sense, but still boring. Haley wanted to play with the numbers, not the methodologies they were collected with.

Let's get the dull questions out of the way first.

Haley was working on the first point—Who should she poll?—when the mysterious next-door neighbor showed up. Haley recognized him a second before their eyes met, from the light scent of citrus and sun-kissed skin that filled her nostrils.

Open-mouthed and wide-eyed, she lifted her eyes and met David Williams' gaze, the same shocked expression mirrored on his face. With his dark hair tucked behind his ears and wearing a simple white T-shirt, faded jeans, and sneakers David looked… well, there was only one way of putting it: *hot*.

Haley cursed under her breath. All of a sudden, a day spent in her room crying seemed like the better alternative.

"Hi," he whispered.

No mocking grin, no challenging attitude. He sat in his chair and, with a few clicks of the mouse, he revived the laptop screen that had gone dark in the meantime.

Haley was still staring at him, ready to pack her things and go, when—eyes still glued to the screen—he added, "We're in a public library, Haley." *Haley.* Not Sunshine or another stupid nickname. "I'm here to work, no need to fidget."

Haley shut her still open mouth and imitated him, turning her eyes to her Mac and trying to concentrate on her homework. She could do this, ignore David and complete her assignments. Haley reread the first question.

Who should she pool?

Well, who was interested in the service levels of the Boston PD and DA? All adult residents of the Boston area counted, for sure. But should she also include non-resident students? Did minors count? Did tourists count? Did David Williams count?

She jotted down the questions—all minus the last one—to justify the inclusion or exclusion of the different groups in her final answer.

What sample size should she set on?

That depended on the margin of error she was ready to accept, and on the desired responses confidence level—to account for the statistical probability of people lying when interviewed.

And what was the statistical probability of her picking the one chair next to David Williams on a campus with more than twenty-two thousand students and over seventy separate library units?

On a regular day, fooling around with percentages and deviations—even for stupid open-ended questions—would've intrigued Haley, but on this particular morning, she was having serious troubles concentrating. What with having to fight the urge to spy on David and what he was doing every five seconds. And what with his distracting aftershave that she could barely— but definitively—detect.

Maybe she should rethink her strategy—start with the heavy-handed numerical problems first, and research the philosophy of statistical analysis later. Yeah, okay. But why was David so blatantly ignoring her? And why was it bothering her if he did? Wasn't it what she always asked of him, to leave her alone? Yeah, which he never did. So why start today?

Careful not to be too obvious, Haley threw a side-peek at David. Contrary to her, he appeared very concentrated on his analysis and was still sorting through his data—*manually*. Could it be that David Williams wasn't the issue? Maybe the nagging at Haley's sides came from the poor way such a beautiful set of raw data was being handled. That must be it. She should show him how models were built, and move on with her homework.

"You're doing it all wrong," Haley whispered.

David turned toward her. "Excuse me?" he asked in an equally low voice.

"Your model." She pointed at his screen. "If you keep doing it like that, it'll take you forever."

"I bet that was the point."

"Uh?"

"My boss dumped this"—David tilted his head toward the laptop—"and five other models to build on me last night saying he needed them ready for Monday morning, but granting me the special privilege of working from home. So I suspect he wanted to make sure I spent every second of the weekend slaving over this."

"You have five more?"

"Yep."

"If you keep going at that snail's pace you'll never finish."

"Thanks for the cheer up." His signature mocking grin finally made an appearance. "Now I'd like to keep working if you don't mind."

"I could show you how to make it a quick job," Haley said. "You'd be done in no time."

David arched both his eyebrows in surprise. "And why would you do that?"

"I can't help myself when it comes to numbers," Haley blabbed without thinking, opening her defenses up for an easy gibe. She'd served it to him on a silver platter.

Haley watched a twinkle appear in his blue eyes, the phantom of the easy retort she was sure they were both thinking: *You mean you can't help yourself when it comes to me.*

She waited for him to rip away, but he didn't. David only smiled, he turned his laptop toward her, and said, "Knock yourself out."

Haley shifted her butt into the chair next to him and avidly set her hands on the almost-virgin dataset. "To do a good job, you need to clean the data first. Then you can start elaborating them…"

"And how do I do that?"

Haley started lecturing him on everything that he was doing wrong, and David stoically took a notebook out of his bag and began to take notes on all his unforgivable model-building mistakes. He watched Haley sort through his first model in less than an hour, asking her to explain what she was doing step by step. And she did, enjoying both the work and the chance to show off her mathematical skills.

Admiring her new model all shiny and pretty on David's screen, Haley felt better than she had all week. With a big smile, she said, "And that's how it's done."

David low-whistled, careful not to make the sound too audible. "Thank you," he said, his gaze more intense than ever.

Despite herself, Haley blushed. "You're welcome. Now I'd better get back to my own work."

She considered returning to her chair, but the gesture would look ridiculous at this point. So she simply pulled her laptop closer and resumed working on her homework questions. And in a weird way, David's nearness stopped bothering her. Haley was still hyperaware of his presence next to her, of his unmistakable scent, but most of the uneasiness she usually felt in his presence had gone. Perhaps because for the first time since Christmas, he'd behaved like a normal person and not a psychopath. The library was a good influence on him.

So Haley spent the rest of her Saturday working side by side with David, answering his questions whenever he hit a snafu in his model building, and even forgetting to eat lunch altogether. When an attendant came to tell them they were ten minutes past closing time already, she was utterly surprised. Even if it was already late afternoon, the sun, being late June, was still high in the sky and the room as luminous as in the morning. So nothing had alerted Haley of the passing of time.

Outside, they stopped on the steps for an awkward goodbye. As long as they'd been cocooned in the protected environment of the library, it had seemed all fine and uncomplicated to sit next to David for an entire day working together. But now that they'd moved outside,

Haley was second-guessing the choice she'd made to stay.

"Hey, I'm starving," David said, breaking the silence. "Want to grab a bite?"

Now, going out to dinner with David was a definite no-no.

"No, thanks." Haley pulled at the strings of her backpack. "I have to go and call Scott," she said, blurting out the first excuse that came to mind. Probably not even an excuse. She hadn't checked her phone all day, library's policies and all, and she really had to call Scott. Also, it was good to remind them both that even if he was thousands of miles away, Scott remained the huge pink elephant standing right next to them.

A dark shadow clouded David's features. "Sure," he said, descending a step. "Well, I'd better get going. Bye."

"Bye."

Faster than she could say *"Williams brothers,"* he was hopping down the remaining steps and sprinting away.

Haley sat on the edge of the porch with a sigh. Unhooking her backpack from one shoulder and rolling it from back to front, she fished her phone out of the small pocket at the base. She unlocked the black screen and saw five missed calls—all from Scott.

Crap.

After plugging in her headphones, she tapped his name.

He picked up on the second ring. "Babe, where have you been? I've tried to call you so many times." He sounded hurried.

"Yeah, sorry. I've been at the library all day, doing homework. I even forgot to eat lunch, and I had my phone on silent."

Why was she leaving out the part where David had been there too?

You know why.

I've done nothing wrong, Haley argued with herself.

Such a pretty little liar…

"Haley, I'm sorry…" Scott said. "I had time to talk before, but I can't now."

"Oh." So the one time she could've had a real, longer-than-a-few-minutes conversation with her boyfriend, she'd spent the day—doing what, anyway?—with his brother and hadn't checked her phone once. Haley wanted to kick herself. "Going somewhere?"

"Yep. Dr. Allen's assistant just called, he's removing a brain tumor today, and I'm invited to watch the procedure."

"Will it last long?"

"Hours, eight to ten." So she wasn't going to hear from him again today. "And the patient will be alert the entire time, isn't it exciting?"

How Scott could get so enthusiastic about spending ten hours watching one person crack another person's skull open and fiddle with their brains—*while the poor dude was awake*—was out of Haley's comprehension, but she tried to sound supportive all the same. "Wow, brain surgery… sounds thrilling."

"Um, listen, I really gotta bounce. Call you tomorrow?"

"Sure."

"Love you."

"Me too."

The words had barely left Haley's lips when the line clicked off. She was tempted to hurl her phone down the steps; it seemed so satisfactory when people did it in the movies. But in real life, it'd only leave her with no phone, or with a seriously damaged one, and she doubted broken technology would lift her mood. A stomach cramp reminded Haley of the skipped lunch. Better get home and order a pizza.

Haley stood up, resenting the warm June sun caressing her face. Never had she hated a summer so much.

Fifteen

Haley

The subconscious is a tricky mechanism, a gray area of the mind that allows individuals to lie to themselves. Haley's most private thoughts must've been safely stored in that gray matter when she walked into the library the following Saturday. How else could she tell herself that she wasn't hoping to catch David there again? That there was no particular reason she'd chosen today—exactly a week after she'd bumped into David—to return to the Loker Reading Room. That, on the contrary, she actively wished for him not to be there. And that when she spotted him seated in the same exact spot as the previous Saturday, it wasn't relief she felt.

Now, part of her suspected there was something fundamentally wrong—or if not outright wrong, at least dangerous in a playing-with-fire way—in her actions. But her subconscious still allowed her enough wiggle room for her to sincerely tell herself that it was okay. That there was nothing wrong with spending time with David. That she hadn't been looking forward to the weekend since Monday.

And that it was for personal hygiene reasons she'd showered that morning—and blow-dried her hair and put lip gloss on.

"Hey," she greeted him.

Yeah, nothing wrong with spotting that same relief reflected in his eyes as soon as they set on hers.

"Hey, Miss Robot."

Miss Robot. No more Sunshine, but not even Haley.

Haley raised both her eyebrows. "I'm not Sunshine anymore?"

"Miss Robot sounded more appropriate."

Haley half-smiled, half-grimaced, loving the nickname but hating that she did.

"I hoped you'd show up," David said, his smile so genuine that it almost shattered Haley's fickle mind barriers. But David's next comment made it okay to ignore the alarm bells. "I have a new modeling challenge for you."

They only shared a common interest in numbers and Excel spreadsheets. It was okay to hang out, nothing wrong with that.

She sat on the chair next to him and asked, "Are you always supposed to work on weekends?"

"It's investment banking, they're not famous for leisure working hours. And it's your fault if I monumentally pissed off my boss."

"My fault, how?"

Someone nearby coughed in a reproachful way, so David lowered his tone considerably when he said, "You had me deliver him a set of six perfectly built models."

"Wasn't that the point?"

"No, as it turns out." David drew his brows close together in a mock-serious expression. "The point was for me to spend every waking hour of the weekend sweating cold, knowing I wouldn't be able to complete the assignment. I should've pulled a couple of all-nighters, and then walked into the office on Monday looking like a properly humbled intern. My boss didn't appreciate the swag…" David smirked.

Yeah, Haley could just imagine the scene. David had swagger enough for ten interns.

She ignored his smug expression and asked, "And you work at this lovely place… because?"

"It's where the best of the best work… it's like joining the military and applying to be a Navy SEAL. The training is going to be a bitch, but if you survive, you're part of an elite force."

"That saves lives and protects the country; you only want to swim in cash."

"It's not about the money…" David pierced her with a stare. "…It's about the challenge."

Haley couldn't sustain that gaze and busied her hands with a stack of notes. "Anyway, is the new model punishment?"

"Boss wanted to make sure I spent the whole weekend working this time. He doesn't know I have a secret weapon."

"And what if I hadn't shown up?"

He held her gaze a moment longer than Haley was comfortable with. "But you did."

Right. Better to bring the conversation back on safer ground. "What's the new model about?"

"What do you know about the stock market, volatility, and risk management?" David challenged.

Haley smiled and cracked her knuckles. "Show me the math."

***

Haley didn't forget about lunch this time—at around midday, hunger bit at her. Still, she was undecided if she should say anything, as she was sure that if she mentioned taking a break for lunch, David would try to join her.

So?

Would sharing a sandwich be all that different from building a model together? Somehow it sounded more compromising—*date-ish.* But when her empty stomach let her know with an angry grumble that it couldn't care less about her moral reserves, Haley asked, "I'm going out for a sandwich, care to join me?"

David lifted a finger toward her, eyes still trained on the screen. "Give me fifteen minutes. I need to finish one thing first."

"O-kay."

Haley looked back at her own screen, off-putted. Not that she had expected David to fall at her feet with gratitude for a simple invite to lunch—well, actually, she had kind of expected it. He should consider himself lucky that after everything he'd done, she was still talking to him—helping him, even. Ungrateful little brat.

Haley was about to put him in his place when his concentrated frown stopped her. He seemed oblivious to her mood shifts. In fact, he appeared so focused on his work that Haley relaxed. Making her wait wasn't personal; Haley was the same when she was so caught up in programming—she didn't see or feel anything else. Not hunger, and definitely not hurt feelings.

Suppressing a sigh, she kept working on her program, throwing him side-glares from time to time—even if she understood the work-frenzy, she was still famished.

A good twenty minutes later, David shut his laptop and they headed out. They grabbed two sandwiches from a kiosk and went to eat them seated at an outside table bathed in the warm July sun. It would've been almost too hot, if not for the cool breeze constantly blowing that made the temperature just perfect.

"You're staring," David said, eyeing her over his half-eaten sandwich.

True, Haley *was* staring. "Who are you?" she asked, narrowing her eyes at him. "And what did you do with the real David?"

"You're looking at him."

"So if you know how to be a normal person, why do you usually act like a jerk?"

"Pardon me?"

Now that she'd started, Haley wasn't about to back down. "Excluding today and last Saturday, you've always acted nasty around me."

"Sorry if I wasn't a jolly good fellow while I had to watch you drool all over my brother."

Haley stopped her hands halfway to her mouth and lowered the sandwich. "Excuse me? You were a poster child for douche central right from the moment you opened the door of your room in Hawaii. I wasn't even with Scott back then."

"I was flirting"—David batted his lashes jokingly while he smiled—"and you were giving me the cold shoulder."

"I wasn't."

"Oh, pluhease." He rolled his eyes theatrically. "You were already so much into my brother there was nothing I could've said to make you change your mind."

Ah, but there was something you could've said, Haley thought, and hoped her emotions wouldn't show on her face.

No such luck. David saw right through her, and when he spoke next, it was as if he'd read her mind. "Not *that*," he said. "I wanted you to like *me,* not a fantasy we both had ages before at a summer dance."

"You still could've been nice," Haley chided, praying she wasn't blushing. Her cheeks flared up whenever she thought about the night of the masquerade. "And why tell me about the ball so much later, then?"

David licked a smidgen of sauce off his fingers. "What can I say? I'm not perfect."

Haley scoffed. "Duh-uh."

"What's that supposed to mean?"

"You really hurt Madison, you know?"

"Oh come ooon, I already told you Blondie was never that into me."

"Regardless of her feelings, you can't expect to yell horrible things at a girl and not have her take them to heart—especially someone as sensitive as Madison."

"I'm sorry, okay?" David scrunched the paper that had been holding his sandwich in a tight ball and hurled it at a nearby bin, his aim impeccable. "I was having a bad day, and I snapped."

Haley swallowed the last bit of her sandwich, then said, "It's not me you should apologize to."

"In a way, I should, though."

Haley didn't reply; she just kept watching him reproachfully. Her expression said: *I'm listening.*

David dragged his chair closer to hers. "I'm sorry I acted like a jerk around you this whole time. It was only because I was angry at Scott for something that happened years ago—and because I was jealous. And I'm sorry I told you about us, about the kiss, the way I did…"

Haley arched one eyebrow.

"And, yes, I'm sorry I made it sound to Scott as if it had just happened. I thought he was going to get mad for a few hours and then get over it. I didn't know he would move halfway across the country five minutes after I told him."

"But you're not so sorry he's gone." Haley scowled.

David's eyes twinkled with mischief and he grinned. "No, I'm not a saint."

Haley wanted to keep glowering at him but found it hard. Her lips seemed to stubbornly want to curl up in a smile.

Features contracted in a mask of innocence, David asked, "Am I forgiven?"

"You're on probation," Haley conceded. Without giving him room to gloat, she got up, walking all the way to the garbage bin to throw away her trash, and added, "Let's go back inside and finish our work."

"At your command, Miss Robot."

Haley made a point to press her lips tightly together and not smile. *Damn,* it was really hard to keep a grudge against the dude. Haley silently cursed herself for being so soft.

Sixteen

Alice

A week later, on Saturday afternoon, Alice knocked on Madison's door.

"Come in," her roommate yelled from inside the room.

Alice opened the door and stopped dead on the threshold. "Whoa, what's going on in here?"

Madison was sitting on the floor surrounded by sheets of printed paper that were scattered all over the carpet in apparent chaos.

"I'm deconstructing *Don Quixote*."

No kidding, Alice thought. "Literally?"

"No, not literally." Madison rolled her eyes as if everyone should know what deconstructing a book meant. "But I need to check different chapters at once to—"

"I'm already late," Alice interrupted, before Madison could launch into a didactic explanation.

Madison stared up at her with a face that said: Well, you're the one who came into my room asking what I was doing... so?

"I wanted to give you a heads-up," Alice explained.

The confusion on Madison's face deepened.

"I'm meeting Georgiana for coffee." Madison's confusion turned to shock, then to shame. "We're going to Crema Café in case you're going out and want to… uh… avoid the place."

"So the newlyweds are back from the honeymoon," Madison said, more to herself than Alice. "They've been gone almost a month… Thanks for letting me know. I'll definitely avoid Harvard Square. Are you going right now?"

"Yep."

"I'll head out with you." Madison stood up, revealing the only tiny circle of carpet not covered in paper. "I could use a break from all this mess." She grabbed her battered leather bag, a paperback from her nightstand, and slipped into a pair of flats. "I'm ready."

"You're taking a break from reading a book by reading another book?" Alice asked, tilting her chin toward the paperback in Madison's hands as they headed out of the apartment.

"This?" Madison scoffed. "This is genre fiction; it's the definition of a break. And I wasn't reading *Don Quixote,* I was deconstructing it. This"—she tapped the book and then pushed the "down" button of the elevator—"is just a story, something I don't have to study, or analyze, or—"

"Deconstruct," Alice offered, entering the elevator.

"Exactly. I can get lost in the narrative without thinking, take a break from everything else, and travel to a different place."

In the lobby, Alice pulled Madison into a hug, saying, "All right, have fun on your break."

"You too."

Madison held the entrance door open for her and they both stepped outside, heading in opposite directions.

***

"Sorry I'm late," Alice said as she arrived at Crema Café.

Georgiana was already there, sitting at a table for two, but as soon as she spotted Alice she got up to welcome her. Her bump wasn't showing yet, but Georgiana still seemed rounder, softer. Not in a weight-gain way. Alice couldn't explain it; it was as if Georgiana's edges had been smoothed, making her sorority big sister a gentler version of her former self.

"Don't worry," Georgiana said, air kissing her. "I got here only a minute ago."

"Wow." Alice smiled, taking in Georgiana's tan and pregnancy glow. "You look fantastic."

"Oh, please. I'm a fat cow." Georgiana sagged back in her chair. "None of my clothes fit anymore."

Inside her head, Alice rolled her eyes. Georgiana was such a drama queen—at over four months pregnant she was barely showing and must've only gained a few pounds, tops.

"A good excuse to buy new ones?" Alice joked. Then she put on her poker face as she asked, "So, how was the honeymoon?"

Georgiana was a close friend and Alice wanted to make sure she was okay without revealing the huge secret Madison had entrusted her with. Plus, there were some truths better left untold. Alice doubted telling a pregnant woman that her husband had almost had sex with a bridesmaid—*and a close relative*—on their wedding day would help anyone.

"Curaçao was amazing," Georgiana said breezily. "The beaches, the weather, the food, the tiny colored houses… everything!"

How about the groom? "And with Tyler? Everything good?"

"Super," Georgiana added, too quickly. She plastered a smile on her face that screamed forced.

"Are you sure?"

"Yeah." Georgiana waved her off. "My husband—how cool is it to say that?—he just worries too much."

"About what?"

"Oh, pfff… the baby, the house, law school. I told him everything is going to be fine, no need to change our plans."

Eyes goggling a little, Alice quickly caught herself and reined in her surprise, schooling her face into a neutral expression. Georgiana sounded as if she believed having a baby wouldn't change a single thing in her life.

Alice cleared her throat and asked, "So you plan to go back to school in the fall?"

"Yeah, why wouldn't I?"

Because of the little human growing inside you who's going to want out in the middle of the school year? *"Won't it be too difficult with a newborn baby?"*

"You sound just like Tyler now. When the baby comes, we'll hire a nanny to help. We can go to the library to study and I can skip a couple of lessons if the baby needs me…"

Georgiana seemed way too optimistic about the impact a baby would have on his parents' lives. But once Georgiana made up her mind about something, there was no changing her opinion, so it'd be pointless to argue with her. "Glad to hear you're not worried."

"I'm not, no need to stress. By the way…" Georgiana leaned forward conspiratorially. "Want to know the sex of the baby?"

"You found out?"

"Had my ultrasound on Monday." Georgiana unconsciously rubbed her tiny bump. "It's a girl," she announced.

"Awww, that's amazing."

"I know." This time Georgiana's smile was positively radiant. "We couldn't be happier."

Without getting up, Alice bump-scraped her chair closer to Georgiana and pulled her into a side hug. "I'm so happy for you."

"A life is growing inside of me." Again, Georgiana's hand went to her belly. "I can't describe how weird and fantastic and unbelievable it feels."

"Sounds overwhelming…"

Georgian's face became really serious. "Sometimes it is, especially how much I already love this little person I've never met. But it's also so scary to know she'll depend on me for everything…"

"Well, you *and* Tyler," Alice said. "Are you worried he's not going to be a hands-on dad?"

"Oh, no. I'm sure he'll be a wonderful dad."

"So how are things between you two, I mean, baby aside?"

"Great, really." The fake smile was back. "He only worries too much."

Alice wasn't sure if Georgiana was purposely refusing to admit there were problems in her relationship—well, marriage—or if she wasn't ready to face the reality as of yet, and was lying to herself. But it was clear the "trouble in paradise" topic was off-limits, so Alice switched subjects completely. "Have you started looking at names yet?"

"Not really. But I bought this on the way here." Georgiana pulled a pink book—titled *Baby Girl Names*—from her bag and opened it. "Want to help me scroll through?"

"Sure."

They both bent their heads over the book and rolled names off their tongues for the rest of the afternoon.

Madison

For her break, Madison chose a coffee shop a good thirty-minute walk away from Crema Café. She ordered a Chai Tea Latte—her favorite—and settled at the most secluded table in the café. With a wall on one side and a huge column on the other, she was screened from the other patrons and could read her escape book in peace.

But after only a few chapters, she got distracted by a female voice on the other side of the column that sounded oddly familiar. A girl had just asked someone why they had to come all the way over here and couldn't meet nearer to campus.

"Georgiana is meeting a friend at Crema Café," a guy replied. "I didn't want to risk running into them."

Madison shrank in her chair—her pulse quickened, and her entire face was suddenly burning with embarrassment. That was Tyler sitting on the other side of the column—as in, Georgiana's Tyler. And now that she'd placed him, it was easy to recognize the other voice as Rose's.

Brilliant!

Apparently, the world wasn't done playing sick jokes with her.

And now I'm trapped.

Madison couldn't get up without them spotting her. And no matter how hard she tried to stare at the words printed in her book, she couldn't avoid overhearing their conversation.

"So, where do you want to start?" Rose asked, an edge audible in her voice. "Hard topics first?" Tyler must've nodded, because Rose kept talking. "What got into you at the wedding?"

Madison wanted to evaporate. She'd never felt more uncomfortable in her own skin—and she'd felt pretty damn uncomfortable in it most of her life.

"I honestly don't know why I did what I did," Tyler said.

"I mean, I get the girl was a blonde goddess…"

A blonde goddess? Were they really talking about her? Madison never thought of herself as beautiful. She usually placed herself in the "not entirely ugly" category, at best.

"It wasn't because of the girl, Rose, she could've been anyone."

Now, that's flattering. Madison scoffed inside her head. It was always nice to be reminded how un-special she was.

"What was it, then?"

"Nothing and everything. Until my wedding day, doing the right thing by Georgiana sounded fine—noble, even. But then I was in front of a minister promising to be with her for the rest of my life, and it all became real. I was married—I *am* married—to a woman I'm not sure I love enough, only because she's carrying my baby."

"Still, trying to sleep with a bridesmaid doesn't seem like an optimal solution."

"Rose, I promise you I'm done with all that shit. I'm never going to cheat on anyone ever again. If my marriage doesn't work out, I'll end it in a clean way. I never want to feel as low as that day ever again."

Makes two of us, Madison thought.

"Whoa, already talking divorce? You've only been married a month. Did the honeymoon go that bad?"

"Not the honeymoon… it's just that I don't recognize my life anymore. We found out on Monday that we're having a girl…"

"Yeah, I heard through the family grapevine," Rose said, probably meaning Ethan had already told her. "Congratulations."

"Thanks."

"Have you talked names yet?"

"No, but I told Georgiana all the names Mark Wahlberg runs off the bear in *Ted* are off-limits."

Rose laughed. "Fun scene."

"Anyway," Tyler continued. "We found out the sex on Monday, and I came home two days later to find Georgiana had transformed your room into a *My Little Pony* nightmare. There's pink everywhere."

Sounds like my cousin, all right.

"Not my room anymore," Rose said. "And you had to decorate it anyway, no?"

"Okay, but she didn't even ask me, she just did it, exactly the same way she got pregnant. Do first, ask later."

Definitely Georgiana's style.

"Have you tried to talk to her about it?" Rose asked.

"No. Honestly, it's hard to talk about anything with her these days. She's completely delusional about the whole 'becoming a parent' thing."

"Delusional how?"

"For one, she has this picture in her mind where we go back to school in the fall like nothing has changed."

"When is the due date again?"

"January 4."

"Okay, so provided she doesn't experience complications, she could complete the fall term with little trouble. But what about winter?"

"Exactly my point. She plans on hiring a nanny and expects everything else to stay the same. We already had endless arguments with me trying to make her understand how it won't be a breeze with a baby crying all night. Or that if she breastfeeds, well, a baby needs to eat every couple of hours. She won't be able to go to class in the morning, forget about our daughter for an entire day, and come back at night."

Madison heard a muffled chuckle.

"Not funny," Tyler protested.

"I know, I'm sorry," Rose said, amusement still audible in her voice. "But I never thought you'd be lecturing me on breastfeeding timing."

"I'm not lecturing you, I'm trying to lecture *her,* but she won't listen."

"Georgiana is the younger sibling, the baby of the house." *More the spoiled princess of the house,* Madison commented inside her head. "She's never been around real babies, so she's being a bit naïve, or over-positive."

"Yeah, but what will happen when stuff gets real?"

"Come on, Tyler, you're not giving Georgiana enough credit. She's a force of nature, and she's not the type to give up. You're in a privileged position already because you don't have money issues. And what Georgiana says is true: you can hire help, and it's going to make a huge difference." Tyler made a scoffing noise, and Rose quickly added, "Let me finish. I know the situation is not ideal, but you can make it work, school-wise. I'm sure HLS has a million facilitations for students who are parents."

"Maybe, but Georgiana refuses to ask the Dean of Students Office."

"So *you* ask. You're going to be a parent, too. Go to the office and ask them yourself, so that when—*if*—Georgiana has a meltdown, you'll already have most of the answers."

"Yeah, I could do that…" Tyler said.

"Duh-uh." Madison could almost hear Rose rolling her eyes. "But how you'll manage school is not the real issue here, Ty," Rose continued. "You and Georgiana are married… I thought you could fall back in love with her, but after the wedding and after talking with you today, I'm not so sure. What do you feel for her?"

There was a long moment of silence until Tyler said, "I care about her… deeply. But more in a she's-going-to-be-the-mother-of-my-child way. I want to take care of her and protect her, but romantically…" Another long pause. "I don't love her that way, not anymore. I'm not in love with my wife and I don't think I'll ever be again…"

And at that moment, something Madison had never imagined being possible happened. For the first time in her life, instead of being jealous of Georgiana, Madison pitied her. Not pity felt in a superior or spiteful way, but genuine, sorrowful commiseration.

Seventeen

Madison

Tyler and Rose spent another good hour chatting and, by the time they were done, Madison's bladder was about to explode. She was sweating cold from the effort of not getting up and running to the restrooms—damn Chai Tea Latte. But if it would've been super awkward to be seen when they'd arrived, making her presence known after eavesdropping on them for two hours was not an option. Madison preferred to pee in her pants—or skirt, in this case. She even forced herself to wait ten good minutes after she heard them leave before hitting the ladies room.

After her break gone wrong, Madison needed a serious pick-me-up, and what better place to lift her spirits than the Widener Library? With its retro vibes and extensive book collection, it was the one place that put Madison in a great mood simply by stepping through its doors.

Madison took the long road to get to the library, cutting across Harvard Yard to avoid having to cross Harvard Square. Georgiana and Alice were probably gone too by now, but with her awful luck, Madison preferred not to take chances.

Jogging up the steps of the tall, rectangular building, Madison already felt more positive. She stepped inside, pausing a second to admire the twin monumental stairs leading to the upper floor, the huge vaulted windows, the dome, and the majestic chandeliers. Neck bent backward, eyes closed, Madison inhaled the scent of knowledge, of culture, of possibility…

She headed directly for the Loker Reading Room, reflecting as she walked if she should try again to finish her escape book or reread *Don Quixote* in a traditional way. It could help to have the whole narrative fresh in her mind before she went back to deconstructing the book. She pulled her—*intact*—copy of the classic novel out of her bag and, nose stuck into the first pages, she strolled on autopilot toward the Loker Room without paying much attention to where she was going. She was so familiar with the building that her feet led her there without much help from her brain.

Still concentrated on the book, Madison lifted her gaze briefly to find an empty chair and sat down, already completely absorbed by the story. No matter if she'd read it a thousand times, *Don Quixote* would forever be one of her favorite books. Madison could identify so well with the protagonist—even if he had a few loose screws. Alonso was a bookworm and a hopeless romantic who'd read so many romances he was convinced he could bring chivalry back and undo all wrongs. And he'd decided to do so under the pseudonym of Don Quixote de la Mancha. Like Alonso, Madison preferred to believe she lived in a more romanticized version of the world and often hoped her life would turn into a fantastic story. The reality of it was so dull…

If I ever write a novel, *Madison thought,* I'm definitely going to write under a pseudonym, something epic. *She sighed.* A girl can dream…

Forty-five minutes later, Madison was close to tears—she was reading the scene where all of Alonso's books were burned and the poor knight, while desperately looking for his library, was told a magician had stolen all the books and made the room disappear—when an outburst of laughter distracted her from the most tragic passage.

With a pretty convincing stare of death in her eyes, Madison's neck snapped up to search for the source of the noise. One thing she couldn't stand was people being noisy at the library. The only two patrons who didn't have their necks bent over a book were a boy and a girl sitting at the farthest table in the back of the room. They were facing the wall, so Madison couldn't see their faces, but something about them sent alarm bells to her brain.

The boy said something, making the girl laugh again. Their tone was low enough for the voices not to carry over to where Madison was sitting, but the girl's laugh was loud, and it was disrupting Madison's concentration. Eyes squinted in reproach, Madison was about to get up to go ask them to keep it down or leave when the girl turned to the right, pushing a lock of hair behind her ear.

Madison gasped as she recognized her best friend. Her jaw dropped open and her gaze snapped to the guy. His face was still hidden, but his dark hair, broad shoulders, and Harvard basketball team T-shirt were dead giveaways.

As she forced her mouth shut, a million questions and ugly emotions crossed Madison's mind. What the hell is Haley doing with David Williams? Why do they look so cozy with each other? How can Haley be nice to him after what he did to me? How dare she do this to Scott?

And then Madison's thoughts turned even uglier. Is she cheating on Scott? With his brother? Are they friends? How can she be friends with David? Does Scott know?

And finally the one thought Madison had never dared voice, not even to herself: *She doesn't deserve him.*

I'm cursed, *was Madison's next realization.* Why do I have to run into all kinds of awkward people and situations today?

Two opposite impulses took hold of her. One side of her wanted to get up and run outside as fast as she could. The other wanted to stay and watch—absorb the evidence of Haley's betrayal toward her, and toward Scott. When Madison's thoughts spiraled from observing from a distance to taking a picture and sending it to Scott anonymously, she realized how poisoned she was by the sheer, bilious envy she felt for Haley and Scott's relationship. She had to leave before she did something stupid and reckless that she wouldn't be able to take back.

Wondering what in the hell had possessed her when she'd thought to get out of the house to *relax*, Madison slammed her copy of *Don Quixote* shut and stormed out of the library.

***

"You're not going to believe the day I had," Madison said to Alice, sagging on the couch next to her in their apartment.

"That bad, huh? What happened? I thought I'd spared you the worst…"

"Maybe you did, but the second and third worst definitely happened."

"What do you mean?"

"Guess who I ran into?"

"Who?"

"Who else would want to steer clear of the place where you were meeting Georgiana?"

Alice stared at her blankly.

"Tyler and Rose, catching up," Madison announced.

Alice's eyes widened in horror. "No!"

"Uh-huh. They had the same idea and chose a café on the opposite side of campus. Pity I was there already."

"Did they see you?"

"No, I managed to stay hidden the entire time and almost peed my pants for the effort."

Alice chuckled. "Oh, gosh. Please tell me about it…"

Madison was just finishing relating the first horrible half of the afternoon when Haley glided inside the apartment as if walking on a cloud.

"Hi, girls," she greeted them. "I'll be out in a sec, save some of the juicy gossip for me." And then Haley disappeared into her room.

Madison narrowed her eyes at the door.

"She's definitely more cheerful these days," Alice said. "I mean, a month ago, when Scott left, she didn't want to get out of bed, and now she's dancing on air."

Now that Madison thought about it, Haley hadn't been heartbroken over Scott leaving for a while. Not that Haley had ever complained openly, but her sadness had been evident to those who loved her. Until Madison had stopped noticing Haley being inconsolable. Because her friend had not been that sad anymore.

"Hey." Alice snapped her fingers to attract Madison's attention. "What's with the pouty face?"

Madison stopped staring daggers at Haley's door and turned toward Alice. "I might know why she's so cheerful."

"And?"

"I saw her at the library getting all cozy with David."

"Williams?"

"Uh-huh."

"Cozy how?"

"They were making a mess of the place with their laughing fits."

"Madison, what are you implying?"

"Nothing, just telling you what I saw. Haley doesn't seem heartbroken over Scott leaving anymore and she's shacking up with his brother while he's gone."

Alice scowled at her. "Haley would never cheat on Scott."

"So what was she doing with David?"

"Maybe they're friends." Alice shrugged.

"Since when? Since she's found out he was the kiss of her life?"

"You're jumping to conclusions and it's not fair."

"I'm not jumping to anything; I'm only saying that something is off here. Has she told you she was seeing David in any capacity: friend or lover?"

"No, but—"

"Me neither," Madison interrupted. "So why hide it if she's doing nothing wrong?"

"I don't know, maybe the topic simply didn't come up?"

"Seriously, Alice?"

"What do you want me to s—"

"Shh," Madison whispered. "She's coming out. Humor me; let's see if she lies about it."

Alice threw her a reproachful stare that said: *We shouldn't pull this bullshit on each other*. But she kept silent all the same.

"So," Haley said, settling herself on the armchair opposite to them. "What are you girls up to?"

"I was just telling Alice what an awful day I had." Madison tried to keep her tone calm, even if all she wanted to do was scream, *"You have the best boyfriend in the world; how can you be so disloyal to him? You don't deserve Scott's love!"*

"Really?" Haley asked. "Why? What happened?"

Madison gave her the short version of her unfortunate encounter with Tyler and Rose, and then asked, "What about you? What did you do today?"

"Oh, nothing special, I was at the library all day, studying."

No mention of David.

Madison flashed an I-told-you-so stare at Alice, who said, "I thought you didn't like the library. Were you working on a group project?"

"No, I was alone," Haley lied through her teeth, and Madison bristled on the couch. "I just needed to get out of the house, and I'm digging the library lately."

The library, or David Williams?

Alice stared at Madison, at a loss for words, Haley had straight out lied, and now even Alice couldn't deny something was up.

Eighteen

Madison

Madison was coming back home from the gym the next day when she spotted David Williams walking toward her from the opposite direction. She froze for an instant and, before he could see her, she turned on her heel and hurried away.

"Hey, Blondie," someone called.

It had to be him; he was the only person in the world who called her Blondie. Madison quickened her pace. She'd be damned before she stopped to say hi to David Williams.

"Oh, come on. I know you've seen me." He was getting nearer. "Would you stop and wait for me?"

Madison turned her head to half-yell, "No, I won't!" then continued striding away.

"Come on, Blondie." David caught up with her and, stepping in front of her to block her path, added, "I only ask for five minutes of your time."

"Five minutes too long," Madison said, crossing her arms over her chest. "What do you want?"

"To talk to you. Can I get you a coffee or something?"

"No. Way."

"Please." He made a cute, pleading face that made him look more handsome than ever. *Bastard.* "I'll get you a Chai Tea Latte. Let me say my piece, and I'll be on my way."

And he'd somehow remembered her favorite drink. *Double bastard.*

Madison frowned. Why was David being so nice? What did he really want? She was ashamed to admit curiosity was getting the best of her. Was it a coincidence that David wanted to talk to her precisely the next day she'd caught him and Haley together? But he didn't know they'd been busted. So what could he possibly want?

Against her better judgment, Madison lifted her index finger in front of her in what she hoped would look like an intimidating gesture. "One drink," she conceded.

"One drink is all I need," David said, heading toward the Starbucks across the street.

Madison sat at a small table outside while he went inside to order. In the ten minutes it took David to get their drinks, Madison second-guessed her decision a million times. More than once, she was tempted to leave, and at one point, she'd almost gotten up.

"You're still here, Blondie," David said when he finally got out, offering her a paper cup and sitting across from her.

Could he read minds now?

Madison took a sip of her drink—delicious, with a pinch of vanilla just as she liked it—and waited for David to talk. Her body language sent a clear message: *not gonna make it easy for you.*

David sighed, once again reading her attitude all too well. "So…"

"So," Madison half-repeated, half-scoffed.

He rolled his cup in his hands a few times before he lifted those impossibly blue eyes and stared right at her. "I wanted to apologize. I've been an asshole to you, and I'm man enough to own up to my mistakes and say I'm sorry."

Madison stared at him, flabbergasted. Of all the things she'd imagined he'd say, somehow *"Sorry"* hadn't made the list. Why was he apologizing to her? Why now? It sounded too good, too decent, to be true coming from certified bad-boy David Williams. A heartfelt, sincere apology was so much out of his character that maybe it *was* too good to be true. A flash of him laughing in the library with Haley passed before Madison's eyes, and she narrowed them at him.

"What's your angle here, David?"

"No angle, Blondie, just a plain and simple apology."

"Yeah?" Madison rested her elbows on the table, leaning forward. "So you're not hoping the second I leave here I'll run to tell Haley what a reformed man you are?"

"As a matter of fact"—David mirrored her posture, leaning forward on his elbows—"I wanted to ask you to keep this conversation private, just between the two of us."

Madison reclined back in her chair and crossed her arms over her chest, studying him for any obvious sign that would give away the lie. She found none. Still, she didn't trust him. "You're telling me not to do something and hoping I'll do it anyway."

"No, I'm not playing mind games here." His nostrils flared. "I'm trying very hard to apologize to you for the crappy way I treated you."

"So why don't you want me to tell Haley?"

His blue eyes pinned her to the chair. "This apology is about *you* and no one else."

"Stop lying, I saw you two getting all cozy at the library yesterday. You're trying to steal her from right under Scott's nose while he's away."

"Blondie, let me tell you something. In love, there's no stealing. People who get 'stolen' *want* to be stolen. If Haley loves Scott and wants to stay with him, there's nothing I could ever do or say to change that. Nothing." David shrugged. "Do I want Haley? Yes. Do I hate that she's dating my brother? Yes. But this conversation between us has nothing to do with Haley. I'm trying to do the right thing by you."

"Why now?" Madison insisted. "You expect me to believe you suddenly had an epiphany and decided you weren't going to be an asshole anymore?"

"As much as everybody likes to paint me as the bad guy, I'm not all bad." David shrugged. "The way I treated you was crap. You're right, I was an asshole—big time. A total dick… Guilty." He lifted his hands as if in surrender. "I went out with you for the wrong reasons and ended things like a complete douche…"

"What reasons?"

David lowered his gaze before speaking up again. "I wanted to make Haley jealous by dating her roommate… there, you have it. The ugly truth, bare and exposed."

"You admitted you want Haley, and that you started dating me only to get at her. How the hell am I supposed to believe this is not all a contorted ruse to look good for her after you screwed up by showing your true colors with me?"

"Because those aren't my true colors," David snapped. "It's what I've been trying to tell you all along. I have a bad temper and sometimes I act like a total jerk. When I get angry, I lash out. I'm aware I'm not always the nicest guy, but this is not all a diabolical plan to look good for Haley. I'm here to say sorry to *you*, and only *you*." He let the words hang in the air a few seconds before going on. "What I said the day we broke up… I snapped, but I don't really think any of the things I said."

"Really?"

David put a hand over his heart. "I swear."

An evil little smile surfaced on Madison's lips. "So you don't think that I talk too much?" She arched an eyebrow at him.

Why could she be this bad ass only with people she didn't care about?

David's mouth curled at one corner, and he smartly avoided the question. "You're beautiful, smart, and any guy would be lucky to have you."

Despite herself, Madison was mollified. "Then why be so mean?"

"Part of my shitty personality, I guess." David rolled his eyes. "Come on, Blondie… Of all people, I thought you'd understand what got me so worked up. Cut me some slack, no?"

"Me? Why me?"

"We both know I wasn't your first pick of the Williams brothers," David said with disconcerting blatancy.

Cheeks aflame, Madison tried to deny it. "I don't know what you're talking about."

"No need to lie, Blondie. I never judge." David's blue eyes seemed to be piercing right through Madison's soul. "The night we met, I saw the way you stared at my brother and I saw the way you looked at them together. Tell me it wouldn't be much easier if Scott was dating a nameless stranger. Or that it wouldn't hurt less if he loved someone you didn't know at all, someone you could hate freely. Someone you could hope he'd break up with as soon as possible. Instead of someone you care so much about." David scoffed bitterly. "The more you care, the more it hurts."

Speechless, Madison stared into his eyes for a long while. In their expressive blue, she could now discern the pain of older and newer scars. Brigitte and Haley, two girls who'd chosen his brother over him. Was that pain so visible in her own eyes, too? Was that why Haley behaved awkwardly around her sometimes?

Madison swallowed and nodded at David. In a weird way, she'd never felt more understood than right now by this guy she'd thought she hated. Not by Alice, and certainly not by Haley. In a thin voice, she said, "Please don't tell him, Scott has no idea."

David nodded back. "Your secret is safe with me, Blondie."

"And stop calling me that."

"All right, Barbie." He flashed her a crooked grin. Guess there wasn't too much reforming David Williams; he'd always play the handsome bastard part. "Are we good?" he asked, standing up and offering her his hand.

"You've earned the benefit of the doubt." Madison took his proffered hand and let him lift her up. Eyes level, she added, "Nothing more."

"That's all I ask." David Williams smiled and pulled her into a comradely hug.

The world was weird.

***

If David Williams deserved the benefit of the doubt, so perhaps did Haley Thomas. Maybe Madison had been too quick in judging her best friend. From the way David had talked about Haley, there was nothing strictly romantic going on between them. Madison still thought Haley was playing a dangerous game, but the jury hadn't rolled a verdict yet.

Oh crap, and now she was thinking like a lawyer. Being part of the Smithson family did leave its legal mark, no matter how hard one tried to escape it.

Demoralized, Madison shuffled a few sheets of paper around on the floor. She was getting nowhere with this research project on *Don Quixote*. She felt like she, too, was fighting against windmills. Not because her enemies were imaginary, but because she was fighting a losing battle.

Madison collected all the scattered pages that had been resting on the floor for the past week and decided to call it a day. Her mind was too crammed with thoughts, doubts, and conspiracy theories for research work. She hadn't told Haley about her little chat with David. Mostly because she still wasn't one hundred percent sure Haley hearing about his redemption had not been his motive all along, and the apology all an act. But she also hadn't confronted Haley about seeing them together at the library. And the number of secrets they were keeping from each other was growing sickeningly fast.

Could a friendship already put to the test by a shared love interest survive so many deceptions? Madison loved Haley, but a small part of her couldn't help hating her too. She wanted to see Haley happy with her boyfriend and at the same time desperately wanted them to break up. Madison wanted everything and the opposite of everything, and it was driving her crazy.

A knock on the door made her lift her gaze from the pages. "Come in," she called.

"Hey." Alice poked her head inside the room. "Haley and I are going to watch an impromptu basketball game, Jack's playing, and then everyone's going for dinner… You coming?"

"Yeah." Madison nodded. "I need a break, just give me five minutes to get ready."

"Sure, we'll be outside."

Madison didn't feel like being in a skirt, so she pulled her dress over her head and hopped into a pair of skinny jeans and a white T-shirt that said: *the book was better.* Flat sandals on, hair up in a messy bun, and she was ready. At the last second, Madison grabbed a paperback from her desk just in case the game got boring.

Nineteen

Alice

"Did you know David was playing?" Madison hissed in her ear.

"No, I swear," Alice replied. They'd just arrived at the gym and already there were troubles. "Jack said the game was among guys on the team, but I assumed he meant *this* year's team."

"Hey, babe." Jack hugged her from behind, making Alice forget about the tension between her roommates. "You made it."

She turned in his arms and fastened her hands behind his neck. "You know I'm a sucker for tall guys in basketball shorts."

Jack put on a cute frown. "And by tall guys in basketball shorts, I hope you mean just *this* guy."

"And who else?" Alice smiled and pulled his face down to kiss him. It still amazed her she could do it whenever she wanted.

"Dude." Someone nudged Jack from behind. "You ready to go?"

Alice broke the kiss and briefly made eye contact with David Williams, who jogged backward calling, "Come on, Jack, we need to get started on some warm-up drills."

It was a two-against-two match and it appeared Jack and David were on the same team. Matt Lucas and Blake Donovan were on the other. Both Matt and Blake were from the Boston area, so they'd stayed for the summer.

Jack turned toward the indoor basketball court, saying, "I'll be right there." Then he whispered apologetically to Alice, "Duty calls."

"You didn't tell me David would be here," Alice whispered back.

Jack's eyes widened. "Why? Is there still drama going on? I thought everything was good." He stole another glance at his teammate. "Did he do something bad?"

Alice was about to answer *"yes"* automatically when she realized that this time, no, David had actually done nothing wrong for a change—unless going to the library had become a crime. "No, not really," she reassured Jack. "But I need to update you on the latest crisis. Now, go bag the game."

Jack stole a peck on her lips, saying, "A kiss for luck," and then joined David.

Still high from the kiss, Alice backtracked to go sit with her friends on the gym floor at the margin of the court. But the moment her butt hit the PVC, she felt like she could cut the tension between her two other roommates with a knife. Madison was scowling at David—and at Haley, too, sometimes—and Haley seemed very busy looking everywhere but in David's direction.

Alice sighed and decided to hit pause and ignore them. She was here to enjoy watching her boyfriend play, not to become an unwilling witness to a silent cat fight. She turned all her attention on him and the game.

Jack looked ridiculously gorgeous running and leaping around, his face set in a concentrated frown every time he tried to outsmart an opponent with his drills or when he prepared for a throw. Alice was grateful to whoever had decided to make basketballs so heavy. The weight had shaped every muscle in Jack's arms, and whenever he wrapped those toned biceps around her... *Get a grip, girl.*

Mid-match, Alice realized she was still positively ogling Jack. Not that there was anything wrong with that, but... After ignoring her roommates for the whole game so far, she turned to check on them. A quick side-glance was enough to leave Alice horror-struck. Haley wore a rapt expression as she watched David run—pretty much the same one Alice must've sported a few seconds ago looking at Jack—and Madison had on an affronted pout as she stared daggers at Haley staring at David.

Alice returned her eyes to the match for a second, appraising the disruptive element. She imagined David Williams as an extraneous molecule ruining a perfect chemical reaction… because, no matter if she had eyes only for Jack, the senior Williams brother was really something to look at tonight—or every other night.

He was dressed in a matching dark blue tank top and shorts and his black hair—pulled back from his forehead by a thin white hairband— seemed so dark it appeared to have midnight-blue streaks in it, which only made his eyes pop more. Like all the other players, he was tall and fit, but David also had that bad-boy aura and lopsided grin that added a charm unique to him. Rugged. Handsome. *Dangerous.*

Alice watched as Jack threw the ball halfway across the court in a quick pass. David caught it firmly in his hands and crouched, only to then spring up in a jump, aiming for the basket without a moment's hesitation—his feet an inch shy of the three-point line. The orange sphere flew over Matt's head, who tried and failed to block it, and landed squarely in the center of the metal ring, almost without touching its borders. The only sign of its passage was a soft swish of the net.

Haley cheered and clapped her hands.

Madison scoffed, visibly annoyed.

"What?" Haley turned toward her, smiling. "We're here to cheer Jack's team, no?"

"Sure," Madison snapped again. "*Jack's* team."

Alice stared up at the gym's roof, wondering if there'd ever be harmony again among her friends. But the night's tension only escalated when the match ended—three games to two for Jack and David—and the guys disappeared into the locker room to take a shower, leaving the girls alone with their unspoken beef.

Haley's anger bubble popped first, and she turned toward Madison with thunder in her eyes. "Care to share why you've had the face of someone swallowing lemons all night?"

"Something *soured* my evening," Madison said.

When Madison turned the bitch on, she could get nasty really fast.

"What's your problem?" Haley asked.

"My problem is what's happening between you and David."

"Nothing is going on between us," Haley said, her tone too angry not to be defensive.

Madison scoffed. "Yeah, keep lying… It's what you do best."

Haley jumped up from the floor. "Excuse me?"

Madison got up, too, and Alice had no choice but to imitate them. She placed herself squarely in the middle to keep her best friends from clawing each other's eyes out.

"I saw you at the library the other day," Madison spat. "You were with *him*, don't deny it. And when I asked you about it you lied."

Haley's mouth fell open, a furious blush spreading on her face, but instead of backing off, she narrowed her eyes and hissed, "If you already knew, why ask?"

Madison crossed her arms over her chest. "I wanted to see if you'd lie about it." She stared Haley down. "You did."

"Girls." Alice tried to inject herself into the conversation. "Why don't we all try to calm down?"

"You tell her," Haley said, pointing at Madison. "She's the one looking down on everyone else from her high tower."

"At least I'm not being shady."

"Neither am I!"

"So does Scott know you hang out with his brother?"

"It's none of your business." Haley glowered at Madison one last time. "I'm out of here," she said to Alice. "I'm sorry, we'll hang next time."

Without another word, Haley stormed out of the gym.

Alice waited for her to be gone before she scowled at Madison. "You really had to do that, didn't you?"

"Why are you glaring at me?"

"Because, Madison, Haley is your friend. *Haley.* You should always be on her side. Even if she was having a full-blown affair with David, you should still be on her side."

"But—"

"No buts. Haley hasn't judged you once, no matter what you did." Alice paused to let her point get home. When Madison's face shifted from haughty to embarrassed, she continued. "I know you're holding her to higher standards because of Scott, but you can't act out this way. It's not fair."

Madison looked close to tears. "Yeah, you're right. None of this is fair. I'm out of here too. See you at home."

In a few quick steps, Madison left the gym, slamming the heavy metal door behind her. Alice sighed and pulled her hair up into a ponytail. She was wrapping the hairband when Jack took advantage of her exposed neck and pressed his lips to the sensitive skin just under her ear, saying, "Hey, where did everybody go?"

Alice turned around; the boys were all showered and ready to go. "The girls left. They had stuff to do at home." She tried to ignore the disappointment on David's face at seeing Haley gone.

Jack arched his brows questioningly, and Alice made a face that said: *Don't ask.*

"Oh, okay."

"Can I still hang with the boys?" Alice smiled.

It was Matt who replied, sporting a wide grin. "You're basically one of us."

Jack wrapped an arm around her shoulders. "Well, let's go. I'm starving." Whispering in her ear, he added, "No more drama for tonight. Deal?"

"Deal."

They all walked out of the gym, and Alice was positively ashamed to be relieved that her friends—and their toxic vibes—had left so that she could enjoy a drama-free dinner with her boyfriend.

Haley

"Haley, wait," came Madison's voice from behind her.

Instead of slowing down, Haley picked up her pace—*Yeah, petty as hell.* But Madison had rubbed her the wrong way tonight. She wasn't sure why she'd lied—*omitted*—to her roommates about being friends with David. But Madison's judging reaction had let her know she couldn't confide in them anymore, or at least not in Madison.

"Haley," Madison called again. "You can't avoid me; we live in the same house."

"Fine!" Haley stopped and spun around. "What do you want?"

Madison caught up with her. "To apologize."

Haley was thrown off by the unexpected declaration but still wasn't ready to give in and just forgive Madison for being the biggest bitch. "I'm listening."

"I'm sorry for going nuclear bitch on you, but why didn't you tell us about him?"

"Are you here to apologize, or to ask more stupid questions?"

"Both. I'm sorry I turned all high-and-mighty on you, but I'm not sorry for calling you out on the lie."

Haley tapped her foot on the curb. "Given your wonderful reaction, can you really blame me for not telling you?"

"Is that the only reason you didn't say anything?"

"I know David is still a sore point for you." Madison kept looking at her, unconvinced. So Haley continued, "And I don't need anyone's judgment for being his friend."

"His friend?" Madison asked. "Haley, you're in denial."

"Denial? How dare you—"

"I saw you together, okay?" Madison shouted, interrupting her.

"So? We were building a model. I help him out with coding sometimes. Big deal. It's not like we were making out or banging each other on the table."

"No, it was so much worse."

"How could it be worse?"

"Because it isn't a sexual thing, Haley, you like him. The fact that he's mystery-kiss-masked guy, that you met him first, changed the way you see him."

"Madison, David and I are only friends. I'm with Scott."

"So why are you doing this to him?"

"And since when have you become the Scott police?"

Madison's cheeks flared red.

"That's what I thought," Haley said ruthlessly. "Guess what? *My* life, *my* boyfriend, *my* choices. Keep your nose out of it."

Pain flared behind Madison's eyes. "Fine. It's just hard to watch you throw away the perfect guy for his douche bag of a brother. When it all comes crashing down on you, don't come crying to me."

Madison pushed past her and kept walking toward their house.

"I won't!" Haley yelled after her.

Twenty

Haley

The fight with Madison nagged Haley's conscience for the rest of the week. So much so that she almost didn't go to the library on Saturday. But the atmosphere inside the house was positively poisonous, and she needed to study, and the library really did help her be more productive.

You could go to a different library, *a voice echoed inside her head.* Well, I don't want to. And I'm not going to let Madison dictate my life.

David was already at their table when she arrived.

"Bad mood?" he asked after taking one good look at her.

"Please don't ask." Needing a distraction, she said, "Do you have any vicious models for me to crack today?"

David dipped his head in a mock bow. "I hear you, vicious model on its way."

After pulling up the file, he offered his laptop to her. Haley sat next to him and happily forgot about Madison's accusations for the rest of the day.

***

As usual, it took an attendant to kick them out for Haley and David to leave the library. They were outside saying goodbye when an insistent vibration in her backpack distracted Haley. She rummaged blindly for her phone until her hand clasped around the slim rectangle. Haley stared at the caller ID on the screen: *Mom*. Weird, they just had their weekly chat last night and her mom never called on a weekend unless something was wrong.

"Mom," she said. "What's going on?"

"It's your father," her mother said, a tremor in her voice.

"Dad? What about Dad?"

"Oh, Haley, he's had a heart attack."

The ground disappeared from beneath Haley's feet. She felt like she was about to faint. "When? How? Is he okay?"

Please let him be okay, please let him be okay.

"He's in surgery right now... Before... we were outside taking care of the garden and I don't know what happened... he just collapsed."

"But what are the doctors saying?"

"The surgeon is optimistic, but they won't tell me anything for sure until he's out of the OR."

Haley made a split-second decision. "I'm coming home."

"Yeah, I figured you'd want to. We're at Mercy Hospital."

"I'll be there as soon as I can."

"How are you getting here?"

"I'll catch a flight or the bus, I don't know."

"Please be safe. I have to call Uncle Tim now."

"I will, Mom, bye." Haley pressed End and immediately googled flights. There were none going out of Boston Logan to Buffalo after five in the evening. "Damn," she cursed. The bus took forever. "I need a car."

She was about to call Madison, when David said, "I'll drive you."

Haley had forgotten he was standing right next to her. "You have a car?"

"Yeah."

"Would you really drive me home?"

"Not would, *am*."

"But Buffalo is a seven-hour drive."

David checked his watch. "If we leave now, we can be there by midnight."

Haley swallowed. "Thank you."

David gave a curt nod. "Do you need to go home to get something?"

"No, I just want to leave."

"Let's go, then."

***

David's car was a midnight-blue pickup. He drove it in silence, following the navigator's instructions on his phone without trying to make small talk. Haley was glad. She wasn't in the mood to talk. She wasn't in the mood to do anything. All she wanted was to get home as fast as possible and be with her family, and David seemed to understand that.

They only stopped once to fill the tank and go to the restroom. David ate a cold sandwich while he drove, but Haley's stomach was too cramped up with worry. David didn't insist on her eating, and once again, Haley was grateful that he let her be. No awkward, *"I'm sorry."* No stupid, *"How are you feeling?"* questions. And no *"You should try to eat something,"* crap. David drove her in silence, the hard resolution of getting her to Buffalo as soon as possible etched on his rugged features.

Haley's mom called again halfway through the trip with the good news that her dad was out of surgery. The doctors had said everything had gone well, and that now they only needed to wait for her father to wake up. The biggest lump eased in Haley's throat; her dad was going to be okay. She would get there in time. She would see him again.

After the call, Haley's phone died, making her curse under her breath. She'd spent too much time on Google, learning everything she could about heart attacks, recovery, and prevention, consuming all the battery. She hadn't thought to buy a charger at the gas station, and she certainly didn't want to stop again now.

"What happened?" David asked, probably worried the call had been bad news.

"My phone died," she said.

"I don't have a charger, but mine still has half the battery if you want to call Scott," David offered.

And, once again, Haley appreciated how much effort it must've taken him to say that.

"You don't need it for directions?"

"It says to go straight for the next two hundred miles. I can manage." David freed the phone from its case on the air vent and handed it to her.

"Thanks." Haley dialed Scott's number and waited on the line. It rang, and rang, and rang… "He's not picking up."

"Probably because it's my number. Try a text."

"No, it can wait until tomorrow." The truth was Haley feared Scott would go into full panic mode and ask her all the questions she didn't want to answer right now. "Mind if I give your number to my mom, in case she needs to get a hold of me?"

David shook his head and didn't add anything else for the rest of the trip.

At exactly ten minutes past midnight, he pulled over near the main entrance of Mercy Hospital.

"Go," he said. "I'll find a parking spot."

Haley didn't need to be told twice; her hand was already on the car door handle. She thanked David again and rushed out of the car and inside the towering building. Her mom had texted her the floor and room they were keeping her dad in, so Haley headed straight for the elevator. She had to meander through a few halls and pass many doors before she spotted her mom standing in the threshold of a room.

"Mom," Haley shouted, probably too loud for a hospital, especially after midnight.

Her mother turned and smiled; she looked tired but relieved. "Monkey," she said, using Haley's pet name.

Haley flew into her mother's outstretched arms and, resting her forehead on her shoulder, she finally cracked down. She started sobbing convulsively while her mother gently stroked her hair, whispering soothing words. "It's okay, Baby Monkey. We got scared, but it's all good now."

"How's Dad?" Haley lifted her head, wiping the tears from her face with the sleeve of her blouse. "Can I see him?"

"The doctors will be out in a minute, and they'll let us in afterward."

While they waited, Haley bombarded her mom with questions, since the doctors weren't around to interrogate. Miranda responded as well as she could. They'd told her that the heart attack had been minor as only a small portion of tissue had been involved, and that they'd been able to remove the clog during the surgery. The prognosis for her dad was a speedy recovery, provided he took better care of his health and stuck to a wholesome diet.

She learned this last part from a young doctor who she'd roped into questioning. "I'll make sure he never touches a slice of bacon in his life ever again," she swore.

The doctor smiled and said, "Seems like Mr. Thomas already has the best care. Would you like to see him?"

"Yeah, can we go in?" Haley asked eagerly.

"Yes, but only for a few minutes. Your father needs to rest right now."

"We won't be long, I promise."

Shyly, Haley entered her father's room. His face brightened as soon as he spotted her on the threshold. He was pale as a ghost, hooked to too many machines to count, with tubes jutting out of his body all over, but her dad was smiling at her.

"Dad." Haley rushed forward, ready to hug him, but stopped just before the bed, afraid of hurting him. She took hold of his left hand instead. "I got so scared."

"I know, Baby Monkey." His voice sounded coarser than usual, but his eyes were alert and full of life. "I promise I won't do it again."

Haley fought back tears again. "We won't let you," she said, wrapping her free arm around her mom and pulling her close. "At the cost of making you a vegan," Haley threatened.

Her father chuckled at the mock threat and pressed his right hand to his chest as if it hurt, which it probably did.

Haley paled.

"Too soon for jokes, Baby Monkey," her dad said. "Now you both go home and have a good night's rest."

"But, Dad, I just got here."

"I'll see you tomorrow, Monkey."

"Come on, Haley." Her mom pulled her closer. "We need to go, your father needs to rest."

Haley planted a kiss on her dad's forehead and left some space for her mother to do the same, before they both walked out wishing him goodnight.

David was waiting for them seated on a chair in the hall outside her dad's room. When he spotted them coming out he got up, his face pale, worried, and tired.

Haley steered her mom toward him and made the introductions. "Mom, this is David, the friend who drove me here."

"We talked on the phone a few weeks ago, right?" her mom said. "Nice to meet you in person, and thank you for bringing our daughter home safe."

David shook her hand. "It's a pleasure, Mrs. Thomas. I'm glad I could help. How's Mr. Thomas?"

"Already well enough to boss us around and order us to go home."

"I'm glad to hear it." David's mouth stretched in a close-lipped smile. "If you're going home"—he scratched the back of his head—"is there a motel nearby you could suggest?"

"Oh, don't be silly." Her mother scoffed. "You're staying with us."

"I wouldn't want to intrude, Mrs. Thomas," David—suddenly the most educated, parents-presentable boy on Earth—said.

"No intrusions." Her mom smiled warmly. "Plus, I came here in the ambulance and we could use the ride home." She spared Haley a wink. "And please, call me Miranda."

"Thank you, Mrs.—Miranda. I'll get the car out front; you can wait for me downstairs." David nodded at Haley, then sprinted toward the elevator.

Haley had followed the conversation between him and her mother with mixed feelings: it was so weird to have David here in Buffalo, meeting her family—*staying at her house.*

"So that's David, huh?" Her mom asked with

a shrewd smile. "*Not* your boyfriend, I take it?"

"David's just a friend, Mom."

"A very good one to drop everything and drive you across the country at a moment's notice."

Haley shrugged. "I guess. Can we go now? I'm really tired."

***

Staring at the roof of her childhood bedroom, it took Haley a long time to fall asleep. The worry-induced adrenaline of the day was still pumping in her blood, but mostly it was the thought of David sleeping in the adjoining room that kept her awake. Haley wasn't sure why the idea made her so restless, but the whole David-in-her-childhood-home scenario seemed so improbable, so out of context. If she'd ever imagined introducing someone to her parents, it had been Scott she'd pictured coming to Buffalo, not David. And definitely not under the present circumstances.

To be honest, the fact that he'd been her hero today wasn't helping either. It was so much easier to disregard David when he was acting like a jerk and hurting everybody. This new knight-in-shining-armor attitude was confusing. It forced Haley to see the good in him, and she couldn't help but like what she saw.

A stab of guilt made her chest contract. These were dangerous thoughts to have, and Haley was too exhausted to even begin to investigate what they might mean. She tried to empty her brain and, after several minutes of tossing and turning, fatigue got the best of her and she finally fell asleep.

Twenty-one

Haley

When Haley came down to breakfast the next morning, David's truck was no longer in the driveway.

"Has David left already?" she asked her mom, accepting a warm cup of coffee.

"Yeah, he got up at the crack of dawn, said he needed to head back to Boston." Her mom placed a bowl of cereal in front of Haley. "Something about having work stuff to finish before Monday."

Haley nodded, realizing just how much giving her a ride had cost David. His boss had given him a ridiculous amount of data to analyze, and even if Haley had helped him a little with the coding on Saturday, he still had plenty to do. And with a seven-hour drive back home, he'd have to work all afternoon and part of the night to finish. Haley felt awful for him.

"Can I say something?" her mother asked.

"I won't like what you're about to say, will I?"

"That depends."

"But you're going to say it anyway."

Her mom nodded.

Sighing, Haley sat on a stool and started eating

the cereal. "Go ahead."

"David… isn't your friend."

Haley dropped the spoon into the bowl, milk splashing all over. "I thought you liked him."

"I do." Her mom paused to grab a towel and clean the mess. "The problem isn't that I don't like him, it's how much he likes you."

"Mom, I already told you there's nothing between us."

"Maybe not on your side." Miranda sighed. "But that boy is in love with you, Monkey."

Haley's pulse raced. "No, he's not."

"You're blind if you can't see it, or you're in denial."

Great. Second time in a week someone told her she was in denial. Well, she wasn't!

Deaf to Haley's protests, her mom continued dispensing unrequested motherly advice. "I know you're very much in love with Scott, but, Haley, if you don't like David that way, don't lead him on. You'll only end up hurting him."

Haley kept her lips stubbornly shut.

"And, Monkey, if you *do* have feelings for him, the sooner you admit it and decide which brother you want, the better for everyone."

Haley refused to acknowledge a word of what her mom was saying. She was with Scott, and they were in love. End of story. "Visitor hours are about to start," she said. "We should get going."

***

Despite her father's many attempts to send them away, Haley and her mom ended up spending most of Sunday at the hospital. Haley had not bought a new charger yet, and she didn't check her messages until later that evening after they'd stopped at a convenience store to buy one and returned home. There were two texts from Scott, and a few missed call alerts.

Without a moment's hesitation, Haley tapped his name, yearning to hear his voice, to be comforted by her boyfriend. In the past twenty-four hours she'd run on adrenaline alone, but now that the worst of the fear had passed, the stress, exhaustion, and weariness were catching up with her.

After three empty rings, Haley knew Scott wasn't going to pick up. She let the call run anyway until the line disconnected on its own. Close to tears, she typed a quick text.

Haley collapsed on the bed, curling into a ball and hugging the phone to her heart. Being in a long distance relationship sucked. She needed Scott, not just his voice. Haley needed to feel his love on her skin. His arms wrapped around her, his lips on hers, their bodies pressed together as they made love. She felt so freaking lonely without him.

While in the midst of contemplating how alone she was, Haley must've fallen asleep, because suddenly she was jolting awake to the sound of *Lovefool* by The Cardigans—Scott's personalized ringtone from *Romeo + Juliet*.

Still groggy with sleep, she unstuck the phone from her left cheek and swept her finger on the screen to answer. "Hi."

"Hey," Scott's voice came warm from the other side. "Did I wake you? I know it's late in Boston, but I saw your text and I thought I'd call anyway."

Haley rolled on the bed to face the ceiling. "I'm not in Boston."

"No?"

"I'm at my parents' house…"

Haley poured out all her anxiety and fear from the past twenty-four hours.

"I wish I could've been there for you," Scott said when she was done talking. "I'm so sorry you had to go home alone…"

I didn't… As her heart skipped a beat, Haley heard nothing else of what Scott said. David had driven her here, and Scott didn't know.

"I didn't come home alone," Haley blurted out before she could change her mind. She lifted up on the bed and tucked her knees under her chin. "David drove me here."

There was a long silence before Scott said, "David?" His tone was suddenly cold and detached.

"Yeah, we were at the library when my mom called. There were no more planes out of Boston to Buffalo and I didn't know what else to do. The train or bus would've taken forever…"

"You were *with* David?"

"No, Scott. We just happened to be in the same place at the same time. I was studying, he was working… Sometimes I bump into him when I go to the library."

"So it was a coincidence he was there when your mom called…?"

"Yes. My phone died last night. I called you from his number to tell you."

"That was you?"

"Yeah."

Scott was silent for a few long seconds. "Why him? Why couldn't you go with one of your roommates?"

"I had zero time to think. David was there, and he offered to give me a ride, and I didn't want to waste any time going home—"

"Did he meet your parents?"

"Just my mom."

"Just your mom, huh?" Scott sounded petty as hell.

"Scott, don't be like that—"

"Wait, is he still there?"

"No." Haley gripped the comforter and closed her fist into a tight ball, crushing the fabric. "He slept here last night, but was gone before I woke up this morning."

"At your parents' house?"

"Yeah, in the guest room."

"Ah, hell, if he was in the guest room."

Blood pounded in Haley's temples. She'd wanted to call Scott to be comforted, not to get sucked into a major fight over David. "Scott, it was nothing shady."

"Yeah, Haley, nothing shady at all. Only, when I left a few weeks ago you swore you hated my brother, and now out of the blue you're bringing David home to meet your parents."

Haley let go of the comforter and massaged her forehead to ease the throbbing. "He didn't meet my parents because my dad is too sick to meet anyone, okay? David was only doing me a favor as a *friend*."

"Since when are you two friends?"

"He apologized a while ago for being a dick, and I guess we've been okay since then."

"And why didn't you tell me?"

"It wasn't a big deal."

Scott scoffed. "Not a big deal, huh? Damn, Haley, first the kiss and now this."

"I called you last night to tell you. It's not my fault you didn't pick up!"

"But it's your fault you were in a car with my brother. There were a million other people you could've asked for help."

"Yeah, maybe. But all I wanted to do was to get home. I thought my dad was going to *die*… I didn't care about anything else at that moment."

"I get it that you were worried—"

"No, Scott, I don't think you're getting any of it."

"What did you expect me to say? To be okay with David playing the hero and you letting him… Why him? Of all people, why did it have to be my brother?"

"BECAUSE HE WAS THERE AND YOU WEREN'T!" Haley shouted, exasperated. She caught her breath, regretting the outburst. "I didn't mean it like that…"

"No, sure." Scott sounded hurt.

Haley felt even more spent and emotionally drained than before falling asleep. "Scott, really, it came out all wrong. I'm just exhausted."

"I should let you get some sleep, then."

Without waiting for a reply, Scott ended the call. Haley didn't have the energy to call him back; besides, she was done arguing and having to justify herself to everybody. She'd done nothing wrong, and if this was the maximum level of empathy Scott could show her after what had happened to her dad, he could go to hell. As tears rolled down her cheeks, Haley grabbed a pillow and used it to choke her sobs until she fell asleep again.

Scott

Scott hung up with Haley and, with a few quick, angry sweeps of his thumb, he pulled up David's number and pressed call.

His brother picked up on the fourth ring. "Ooh, hello, to what do I owe the pl—"

"Stay the hell away from my girlfriend, David," Scott yelled into the phone.

He was still trembling with suppressed fury after speaking with Haley, and he needed to vent his anger on the one person responsible.

"Calm down, Scotty, you seem to be in a bit of a rage."

"How dare you—"

"What? Help your girl at the moment she needed it the most? What are you mad about, exactly?"

"Must've been nice to play the hero. Pretending to be a friend when you're not…"

"I never kept my intentions secret, brother."

"Have some decency. Haley is *my* girlfriend."

"Oh, I see. So your morals have shifted, now? Isn't a brother's girlfriend fair game for you? What changed?"

"Cut the crap, David. I don't want to get sucked into the Brigitte fight again. We were freaking teenagers, get over it."

"Oh, using the I-was-too-young excuse? Have you finally outgrown the I-didn't-know one? Come on, Scotty, you can do better than that."

"What were you doing with Haley, anyway?" Scott felt guilty for not trusting Haley's version, but when his brother was involved, he lost all rationality.

"I bumped into her at the library. I'm sure you're not so insecure that you don't even want your girlfriend *talking* to other people."

So Haley had told the truth. Still, Scott wasn't satisfied. "You didn't just talk to Haley, you drove her home for seven hours, met her parents, and slept at her childhood house."

"And what should I have done, genius? Let her drive home alone in the state she was? Let her wait the night for a flight? Put her on an eleven-hour bus ride? What? She tried to call you to tell you; pick up your phone next time."

Scott cursed himself for the umpteenth time for not answering the call. He'd seen David's number flash on his screen and had ignored it.

By his silence, David must've known he'd struck a chord, because he twisted the knife deeper. "By the way, it's always nice to know I can count on you in case I'm in an emergency."

"Spare me the lecture. You're a dick."

"I'm a dick? You're mad because you weren't there when Haley needed you the most."

Scott's grip on the phone tightened. "And whose fault is that?"

"Not mine. I'm not the one applying to cross-country internships before checking if my girlfriend is okay with it."

"The only reason I took the internship is that you lied to me."

"Technically, I didn't lie."

"Technically, you're an asshole."

"Scott, let me give you some brotherly advice: your girlfriend just went through the most horrible night of her life and, instead of comforting her, I assume you've been a petty bitch…" Scott hated when his brother was right. "Do yourself a favor and get over your wounded ego. As much as I hate to say this, Haley needs you right now—a better version of you, at least."

"Why are you telling me this?"

"Because I care about her." David didn't just

care about Haley; it was in the tone of his voice. He was in love with her. This wasn't a petty revenge or him being a jerk for the heck of it. They were in love with the same girl, *again.* The realization hit Scott in the stomach like a sucker punch. "And I don't want you to make my job too easy," David added, switching back to being an ass. "Wouldn't be fun otherwise."

Scott ignored the jibe and said what was really on his mind. "I'm sorry this happened again. I didn't know you had a past with Haley when I met her."

"Don't go soft on me, brother." There David was, doing it again—hiding his real feelings behind sarcasm. "If you don't mind, I have a ton of work to finish for tomorrow, and it's the middle of the night here."

"David?"

"Yeah?"

"Thanks for making sure she got home safe."

"You're welcome."

Twenty-two

Haley

Staring at the writing on the screen, Haley
hesitated. The message was several minutes long.
What would Scott say? Would he break up with
her? Haley couldn't stomach the idea. She stared
at the message for a while. Then, with trembling
fingers, she opened the recording and put the
phone on speaker.

*"Hey, it's me... I know you probably hate me
right now, but I need to say this... I'm so sorry for
last night. You were down, and I acted like a jerk.
I should've been there for you, and instead, I made
an awful situation worse. I feel like shit thinking
about how I behaved...*

*"Sorry I didn't get how hard it's been for you
and your family... It's just that after basically
living in a hospital for a month, a heart attack
begins to sound almost like a bad cold. And I'm
not saying it was, I'm trying to explain why I
might've lost perspective. Haley, I... I...*

"What I'm trying to say is that I've been a total dick. I thought about what was best for me and not you. After hanging up with you, I called David to yell at him, too… and I have to say, he put me in my place. Totally in a David-ish way…" Scott chuckled in the recording. *"Serves me right, I guess. In the end, I'm glad my brother was there to drive you and make sure you got home safe, and I'm so glad your dad is okay…*

"Haley, please forgive me. I'm so, so sorry…" Scott's voice sounded choked. *"I hope you're willing to give me another chance. I love you…"*

Without checking the time—in either city—Haley called him back.

Scott picked up on the second ring, sounding half-asleep. "Hey."

"Did I wake you?"

"I'm glad you did, I was having a nightmare anyway."

"What nightmare?"

"One where my perfect girlfriend broke up with me for being the greatest idiot."

A smile crept on Haley's lips. "Funny you said that, I was having the same bad dream."

"Any guy would be crazy to break up with you."

"So you're no longer angry with me?"

"I consider myself lucky you're still talking to me. Can we pretend last night never happened?"

"Yes… yes!" Now Haley's smile stretched so wide her cheeks hurt.

They were still on the phone an hour later when her mom called from downstairs, "Haley, we have to leave in twenty minutes… Are you up?"

"I'll be right down, Mom," Haley shouted back, and then added into the speaker in a normal tone, "I have to go, talk later?"

"Okay. How long are you staying in Buffalo?"

"Until tomorrow, or Wednesday at the latest. I wrote to my professors to explain the situation, and they all said it'd be okay to skip a couple of classes. But it's finals week next week, so it's back to Boston even if I don't want to."

"Your dad will be fine."

"Yeah, everyone keeps telling me so. But I'd still prefer to spend more time here."

"HALEY!" An impatient shout drifted up from the bottom of the stairs.

"My mom is going crazy," Haley said. "I really have to go."

"Okay. Say hi to your parents and call me when you get back from the hospital."

"Will you be home?"

"Dr. Allen's schedule is all right today."

"Okay, gotta go. Love you."

"I love you too."

When Haley and her mom arrived at the hospital, there were two huge flower bouquets in her dad's room. Both were from Scott. The one for her dad was white, yellow, and blue—the Buffalo Sabres' colors, he was a huge hockey fan—and the other was red roses for Haley.

"Seems like our Baby Monkey is dating a very proper young man," her dad said with a huge smile on his face.

"Yeah." Haley opened the card—it simply said: *Sorry, I love you*—and joined her dad in smiling. "The best."

***

After a thousand reassurances from the doctors that her father wasn't going to suddenly get worse, but only better, and a million promises from her mom that she'd put him on a healthy diet and make sure he rested, Haley was ready to leave.

She caught the last flight from Buffalo to Boston on Wednesday night, and both Madison and Alice came to pick her up at Logan Airport in Madison's car. From the moment Haley spotted her two best friends' worried faces as they waited for her at the arrival gate, she knew that even if there had been tension between them lately, they were going to be fine. No matter the petty squabbles over boys, they'd always be there for one another.

As soon as she passed the barrier, Madison and

Alice ran toward her pulling her into a crushing three-way hug. They brought her home and cuddled her to death until all three were too tired to keep their eyes open. It became even clearer how worried her roommates had been when Alice tiptoed into her room to leave a half-asleep Blue with Haley. The tiny bundle of fur was the ultimate pick-me-up of the house. He was the sweetest bunny, he loved to be picked up, to cuddle, and if scratched behind the ears he'd start to purr like a cat.

Haley thanked her friend and gladly snuggled Blue close to her chest, falling asleep to the comforting sound of his gentle bunny-purring.

The final days of class were busy enough not to let Haley's mind wander too far over what could've happened to her family. Over what would eventually happen when her parents became old. If she had had nothing to do, she might've slipped down a rabbit hole of catastrophic scenarios filled with hospitals and tubes and sick people.

But before she had time to notice, it was the weekend again. As she jogged up the steps of the Widener Library early on Saturday morning, Haley kept moving her hair around—side to side, up in a bun, down again—and readjusting the straps of her backpack. This would be the first time she'd seen David after he'd driven her home.

Would he even be there? Would the easy, we-play-around-with-coding-sometimes relationship they'd established over the past month be changed? Scott had said he and David were okay now, but was he telling the truth? Or only saying what Haley wanted to hear?

When she reached their usual table, David wasn't there, and the pit of hard disappointment that hit Haley low in her belly scared her to death for a moment. But she didn't have time to analyze her gut reaction to David being missing because she soon heard his voice come from behind her, "Hey, Miss Robot, you're back."

She turned, at a loss for words. There were a million things she wanted to tell him—to thank him for making a horrible day slightly less horrible, for being her hero without asking for anything back, for making Scott understand instead of trying to work him up more.

The emotions must've shown on her face, because David's features turned serious—his signature lopsided grin evaporated, and the twinkle in his eyes switched from playful to intense.

"Come here." David pulled her into a hug.

Haley didn't want to ask herself why it felt so good to be in his arms, if it was right or wrong, or what it meant. For a few instants, she let herself live in the moment. She was starved for affection and she needed a comforting hug.

David let her go, saying, "Your dad will be fine, he gave you a scare, but it's over now."

"Right." Haley very un-sexily sniffled. "My mom has already gotten rid of all the salt in the house."

"No." David made a mock-scared face. "And what if the Sanderson sisters were to attack?"

Haley smiled. "I didn't take you for a *Hocus Pocus* fan." Weird how David always managed to make her smile. "We'll think about it when Halloween comes."

"You've got work to do?" David asked, pulling back a chair to sit down.

Haley imitated him. "Yeah, finals begin on Monday." She sat down and sighed. "Sadly, no laptop for me today."

"Me neither. What did you do?"

"Why? You did something and they took your laptop away?"

"My boss was so pissed off I completed the last assignment that he moved me to analog crap."

Haley lowered her gaze, taking more time than necessary to fish her notebook out of her bag. "I'm glad you managed despite the seven-hour detour."

"I had a good teacher." David winked. "What's your excuse for being technology free?"

"A crazy professor." Haley shrugged. "He says we completed enough coding assignments with our homework and midterms. For the final, he wants us to become the computer."

"Meaning?"

"We have to show we not only know how to code, but also that we understand what each command triggers inside a machine. So we have to do all the corresponding calculations by hand."

"Because?"

"Apparently so that if humanity was ever caught in an apocalypse that destroyed all existing machines, then we'd be able to program new ones from scratch."

"Awesome." David grinned.

"Lame." Haley rolled her eyes. "What's your poison for today?"

"One of our clients was stuck in the Middle Ages and kept physical-only books. And guess who has to check they were dematerialized correctly?" David dropped two gigantic piles of paper on the table. "Copy of the original against a printout of the digitalization."

"Isn't that a waste of a Harvard-graduated brain?"

"It's not about the sophistication of the work, it's about letting me know I'm at the bottom of the food chain and testing if I'm a quitter."

"Are you?"

David flashed her one of his intense, electrifyingly blue stares. "When I want something, I never give up."

On that note, Haley blushed and decided it was probably better to study for her exams. Pen in hand, she bent her head low over her exercise sheet and started working. David did the same next to her.

***

Half an hour before closing time, a dark shadow crossed over the library.

Haley lifted her gaze to the ceiling. Where there had been bright squares of light a few moments ago, now there were only dark-gray patches.

"Maybe we should go before it starts raining," she said.

"Too late for that, Miss Robot," David said as the first raindrops spattered the roof. "Are you finished?"

"One exercise left. You?"

"It'll take me all weekend to finish. No cheating this time." David shrugged and went back to work.

"I'm done," Haley announced ten minutes later. "We should get going; it seems like it's getting worse."

Now there was a steady hammering of water hitting glass.

"Yeah." David dropped his pen and stretched

his right hand. "Library's closing in fifteen minutes anyway."

They both packed their things and headed downstairs.

The moment Haley pushed open the lobby door, a strong gush of warm wind pushed back against her, carrying a spray of water in its wake.

Head bent low against the wind, Haley stepped out. Despite it being five in the afternoon, there was so little light that the day had turned to night hours early. Dark clouds the color of lead crowded the sky, rain unloading off them in large, fat drops—a perfect summer storm.

"I don't have an umbrella," Haley called, having to shout to be heard over the rolling thunder. "Do you?"

"No," David yelled back. "And I don't care."

He hurried past her out of the cover of the library porch and ran down the steps. When he reached the bottom, he tilted his face up and closed his eyes. In a matter of seconds, he was soaked.

"What are you doing?"

David looked at her from across the street, he was walking backward toward the center of Harvard Yard. "Come here. It's only water."

Haley didn't know what possessed her, but she did as he asked. She ran off the porch and joined him in the middle of the park. The sensation of the rain on her skin was electrifying as she spun on her toes, arms opened wide. Haley looked upward and laughed and laughed, unable to stop—until she pirouetted right into David's arms. The smile died on her lips as he caught her wrists and held her hands close to his chest, leaning his head down…

She tried to pull back, a ragged breath catching in her throat. "David, don't."

David's lips brushed her forehead in a soft, wet kiss. "I wasn't going to," he whispered. "The next time we kiss, you'll want to just as much as I do now…"

There. Haley couldn't pretend anymore that David didn't have feelings for her. She lifted her eyes to meet his. "David, I care about you, but I'm in love with Scott. That's never going to change."

"Never is a long time. You can't deny that what we've been doing here means something…"

"David, we're friends." Haley tried to pull back again, but he wouldn't let her go.

"You're a liar, Haley." David's eyes flared up with dark emotions. "You're lying to me, and you're lying to Scott, and most of all you're lying to yourself."

"Don't do this to me, David, please don't."

"I'm not doing anything, only telling you how things are. I won't lash out again or try to do stupid things to make you jealous, and I won't try to get between you and Scott. But I want you to know how I feel. I want you to know that when you're ready to admit that you feel the same, I'll be there." He tightened his grip on her hands, but not in a way that hurt. "I won't go away, Haley. I'll always be here for you." David pulled her wrists up and kissed her knuckles. Then he locked his impossibly blue gaze on her. "I love you."

Twenty-three

Haley

Walking home under the pouring sky, Haley didn't feel the tickle of the droplets landing on her face, or the rain soaking her clothes and sneaking down her spine. All she could feel was the echo of David's words: *I love you.* The intensity of his stare as he said them, and the ghost of his lips on her forehead.

Okay, let's calm down, Haley thought. It was perfectly normal not to remain indifferent when someone declared his undying love in the most romantic rain shower ever. But David wasn't just anyone, he was David. He was the boy in the mask, the one who'd saved her at her darkest moment.

Haley vowed to avoid him for a while. She didn't have the mental ease to deal with his—*or her*—feelings right now. Luckily, their casual little ritual of spontaneous Saturday meetings at the library had no more reason to exist. Summer School was over, and there were no more excuses—*need,* it had very much been a practical need—for Haley to go to the library.

True to expectations, finals week kept Haley

busy. Between last-minute revision sessions, the amount of work she had to recoup from the four days she'd spent in Buffalo, and the exams themselves, her mind didn't have much time left to dwell on boys telling her they loved her in the rain.

On the first Friday in August, Haley came home from her last exam feeling positively drained. And she wasn't done yet; she still had to pack her bag, as she was leaving for Buffalo the following day. But all she wanted to do was curl up under the blankets—maybe stealing Blue from Alice again—and sleep.

Her roommates had different plans. They'd both been waiting for her to get home, and ambushed her as she entered the apartment, shouting, "Happy birthday!" and blowing into a pair of ridiculous party blowers that made a hideous noise.

Oh, no. No. No. No. The last thing Haley wanted was a birthday party. She hoped the surprise ended at the blowers and chocolate-glaze cupcake with a single candle on top that Madison was now bringing forward.

Forcing a smile on her face, Haley said, "Thank you, guys. You didn't have to." She was about to blow the candle when Madison stopped her.

"Wait, you have to make a wish first."

I wish my bag will magically pack itself, and to have an early night tonight.

Haley was a practical girl.

"Done," she announced. "Can I blow now?"

"Knock yourself out." Alice smiled.

They all cheered as the tiny flame blew out. Alice promptly took the chocolate cupcake away and cut it into three slices, doling one out to each of them.

Haley took a bite and closed her eyes, savoring how creamy and delicious the cake was. "Umm, this is heaven."

"Yep," Alice agreed, scarfing down her slice.

Madison was still licking her fingers when she peeked at her watch and announced, "Come on, Haley, you have two hours to shower and get ready. Then we're taking you out to celebrate."

Haley suppressed a groan and tried to put a conciliatory expression on her face. "Guys, I'm super thankful for the surprise, but can't we just stay in and binge watch romcoms?"

Madison threw Alice an I-told-you-so stare before saying, "Absolutely not. We have plans."

"But I still have to pack my bag to go home, and I leave super early tomorrow."

Madison looped her arm under Haley's elbow and steered her toward her room, saying, "Which is why we took the liberty of packing for you." Madison pushed the door open to reveal Haley's bag standing open on the floor, packed to perfection. Clothes, shoes, and makeup cases were arranged in tidy rows, and all the space was occupied with the maximum possible efficiency. Haley had never seen a suitcase better organized.

"Now, chop, chop." Madison playfully spanked her to prompt her to enter the room. "We're on a schedule."

"Okay, okay." Haley rolled her eyes and pushed Maddie out the door.

She started donning her clothes and, still in her underwear, she grabbed a clean towel to go shower. With a sigh, she threw a wistful glance at her packed-to-the-brim bag. Well, at least one half of her birthday wish had come true.

***

When she came out of the steaming shower, she found the girls eating pizza at the kitchen bar.

"Wait, are we staying in or going out?"

"In for food," Madison said. "Out for fun."

"We're meeting the others at a bar in downtown Boston," Alice explained. "But we wanted to eat first and avoid getting drunk on an empty stomach."

Haley hoped to avoid getting drunk on any kind of stomach, and she also wondered who "the others" meeting them downtown were. But the pizza smelled delicious, so, with one pink towel wrapped around her body and another one around her head, she sat next to Madison and grabbed a slice.

For three girls, the giant pizza sitting in front of them disappeared alarmingly quickly.

Brushing her hands together to get rid of the crumbs, Haley asked, "What's the dress code?"

"Dressed up," Alice said, shrugging apologetically as if to say: *not my fault.*

"High heels?" Haley asked, disgruntled.

Both her roommates nodded.

"Are we going to walk?"

"Hell no," Madison said. "We'll call an Uber as soon as we're ready and"—she looked at her watch—"we should get a move on."

They all hopped off their respective stools and paused in the hall.

"Meet again here in half an hour?" Madison asked.

They all nodded and disappeared into their rooms. But of course, in less than five minutes they all ended up in Madison's room, exchanging makeup, curling each other's hair, and trying on outfits.

Haley opted for a white dress with spaghetti straps and an empire waist, Madison for a colorful, flowy dress, and Alice for a classic little black dress. And, voilà, they were only slightly late when their driver dropped them off at the designated bar downtown.

Inside, their usual crowd of friends was waiting for them. Mostly girls from their sorority and guys from the team: Matt Lucas, Blake Donovan, Jack… and, of course, David Williams. He was drinking a beer with his elbow propped against the bar, talking to Becky, another soon-to-be-senior Kappa Kappa Gamma.

Becky had a bit of an easy-girl reputation. She'd slept with Jack the previous year—way before he was with Alice—and from the way she was flirting with David now, she looked like she wouldn't mind going home with him tonight.

Haley grimaced involuntarily. The idea somehow didn't sit well with her. Not so much what—*who*—Becky did or didn't do. Everyone male or female was free to have sex or not have sex with however many people they wanted. But the certainty that she didn't want Becky and David to sleep together tonight struck Haley like a bolt of lightning, sending a weird current down her spine.

He lifted his gaze and their eyes met, causing another stream of electricity to course through Haley's body. This was the first time they'd seen each other after David had told her he loved her. Even at a distance, and even in the faint lights of the bar, the blue of his eyes sparkled. David's mouth curved up at one corner and he waved.

"What are you looking at with that long face?" Madison asked, and then followed Haley's gaze to the bar. "Who the hell invited *him*?"

"Come on, Maddie." Alice rolled her eyes. "He's friends with everyone we know, and he's Haley's friend, too. Right?" She turned to her for confirmation.

Haley blushed profusely and nodded, hoping the dim lights would cover her flush.

"Whatever," Madison said, and marched off to the opposite side of the room to go talk to Matt.

"I need a drink." Haley plastered a smile on her lips. "Join me?"

"Can't wait for a Cosmo, they make the bestest here." Alice linked her arm with Haley's and they joined Jack and Blake in the line to order.

There, Alice let go of Haley and wrapped her arms around Jack's waist, a megawatt smile brightening her face at once. "A Cosmo for your girlfriend and another one for the birthday girl."

Jack turned around, his smile matching Alice's, and bent down to steal a kiss. "Two Cosmos for the ladies on their way."

Haley felt a little pang of envy. Their happiness made her miss Scott so much more. It'd be another three weeks before he came back, and it still seemed like an eternity. Haley looked away from the happy couple, and her eyes landed on Madison next, guilt replacing envy at once. At least she had a boyfriend who adored her and who'd be here soon; what about Maddie?

Following Madison with her gaze as she moved across the room, Haley was surprised to see her friend stop next to David. At once, Becky made herself scarce and Madison and David began to talk in hushed tones. He was smiling, and she was scowling—without looking really mad.

For the first time, the reality that Madison had actually had sex with David—*multiple times*—struck Haley like a blow. They had that intimacy peculiar to ex-lovers. Madison looked too comfortable for her own good.

Everything Madison did lately confused Haley. First she was dating David, then she was in love with Scott. And after David had broken up with her in the worst possible way—if one was to believe her version of the story—there she was talking to him as if they were a pair of old friends. From the way she acted whenever he showed up in their group, Madison seemed to still hate David, so what business did she have talking to him?

Haley wished she could hear what they were saying.

Madison

Madison had not asked Haley a single question about her emergency road trip with David. If Scott knew and had nothing against it, neither did Madison. Even if she suspected David was gaining too many points with Haley. But their friendship had been on the mend since Haley had come back from Buffalo, and Madison didn't want to risk ruining this newfound balance with indelicate questions.

But there was nothing wrong with probing the other party interested.

"Still playing the good boy part?" Madison asked.

"Not playing any part, Blondie." David smirked. "It's not my style."

"And how's your diabolical plan to steal your brother's girlfriend going?"

"Why? Hoping I'd get a move on?"

"That's not—" Madison started defending herself, but then she noticed David's amused face and swatted him instead. "You're still a jerk."

"Oh, come on, Blondie, I'm only teasing you a little."

Madison scoffed. "Why are you here?"

"To wish Haley a happy birthday. Is that against the law?"

"David, I know you… You have the charm on."

"Are you charmed?"

"I'm immune."

"Ouch." David brought a hand to his chest. "Now you're hurting me, Blondie."

Madison scowled at him. "I will if you mess with Haley."

David arched an eyebrow. "Am I still on your watch list?"

Madison wasn't sure. "I'm glad you were there for Haley during the crisis with her dad, but I'm not sure your gesture was one hundred percent selfless."

David made a cute, I'm-innocent face. "No?"

"Stop playing dumb. I bet you enjoyed being the hero."

"Is that how Haley describes me now?"

Madison smiled despite herself. "You're impossible."

"And you're charmed."

"Am not."

David smirked but didn't say anything.

Madison chewed on her lower lip.

"Come on, Blondie, spit out whatever you're dying to say."

"David, I know you care about Haley. But sometimes the best way to show someone you care about them is to back off and let them be happy with someone else."

"The way you do, Blondie? And how much good has that done you?"

"Now you're being mean again."

"No, I'm telling the truth, just like I always do. Now, if you'll excuse me…" He pushed past her and disappeared into the crowd.

Madison watched him go, not knowing if she still hated him to death or if he was growing on her.

Twenty-four

Haley

Fed up with watching David and Madison flirt—it definitely looked as if they were flirting—Haley excused herself and went to the restroom to calm down.

What the hell?

Madison had even smiled at him at one point. Funny way to show her hatred. And what about David? So much for being in love with her, and for promising he wouldn't try to play mind games or make her jealous… And why was it that simply seeing him talk to one of her friends made her jealous?

They used to be together.

So? What place do you have being jealous?

Haley shook her head. *None.*

Still, she couldn't shake the feeling. And it annoyed her.

Haley entered the restroom and stood in front of the mirror. She didn't really need to use the toilet, so she decided to fluff her hair and reapply her cranberry lip gloss.

On top of everything else, Scott still hadn't called to wish her happy birthday. Sure, he'd sent a cute message with a silly picture that morning, but nothing else all day. He was probably locked in an OR, but Haley wished he'd make the effort to find the time to call.

When she could no longer pretend to be fixing her hair, Haley dropped her lip gloss in her clutch and headed out, checking her phone for new messages. There were none.

"Hello, Birthday Girl." David's voice startled her halfway down the corridor to the main bar.

Haley lifted her gaze from the screen to find him propped against the wall, arms crossed over his chest. He'd clearly been waiting for her.

"What? Are you stalking me now?"

"Oooh." That infuriatingly sexy grin spread on his lips. "Feisty, aren't we? I like it." He lowered his gaze to her legs. "The heels, too."

"What do you want?" Haley didn't know why she was being so rude.

"Only to wish you a happy birthday."

"You could've done it as soon as you saw me."

"True." David pushed himself off the wall and searched the folds of his jacket. "But I wanted a little extra privacy to give you this." He took a small box out of an inside pocket.

"What is that?"

"A birthday gift, obviously."

Haley softened at once. "David, you can't give me gifts."

"What? Now a *friend* can't give you a present for your birthday?"

Haley scowled at him. "A *friend* could. Is that what we are… friends?"

Lips curling up only at one corner of his mouth, David said, "This is a one hundred percent friendly gift." He handed her the small box.

"What is it?"

"Open it."

Haley did, and gasped when she discovered a stunning dark-silver locket inside. It was an engraved oval in a Gothic style, beautiful and perfect. "David, thank you, it's gorgeous. You shouldn't have."

He really shouldn't have.

"May I?" he asked.

Haley gave him the necklace and turned toward the wall, holding her hair up. David came closer, looping the necklace around her neck and fastening it at her nape. His fingers grazed her skin, and shivers spread down her spine. Haley had to make an effort not to shudder under his touch.

"Now," he said, letting the chain fall in place. "You wouldn't think I'd buy you jewelry, right?"

Haley scoffed, facing him again. "No?"

David reached for the pendant. "It's a secret container." He flipped the locket open to reveal a hidden USB key inside. "Thirty-two gigs of data at your disposal anytime you need it, Miss Robot."

Haley smiled. This really was the perfect gift for her. "A girl never knows when she might need extra gigs."

Just then, Haley's phone started ringing. *Lovefool.*

"It's Scott," she said. "He hasn't wished me happy birthday yet."

David's smile faltered slightly. "I'll leave you to it. See you later."

Haley watched him go, filled with mixed emotions. She waited until he'd turned the corner to pick up.

"Hey," she breathed into the mic.

"Hey, are you out celebrating? I can barely hear your voice over the music."

In the hall the music was less loud than in the main bar, but it was still loud, especially to talk over the phone.

"Give me a minute; I'll go outside… Here. Can you hear me now?"

"Loud and clear. Happy birthday!"

"Thanks."

Tires screeched on the concrete, distracting Haley. She lifted her gaze and spotted a familiar truck crossing the road and merging onto the MA-28 toward Cambridge. She only got a side-peek at the driver, but enough to recognize his slight frown. The same one he had on whenever he was concentrating on the road—she should know, she'd spent seven hours watching him drive not long ago.

Haley's chest contracted a little at seeing David go. Was he mad at her? He couldn't be. At least, he didn't have any right to be. Maybe it was better this way for everyone. On impulse, Haley's phone-free hand closed around the locket dangling from her neck.

"Haley, are you still there?" Scott's voice brought her out of her trance.

"Yeah, sorry. What were you saying?"

"I was asking if you're having fun."

"Yeah, the girls organized a surprise party, they made me a birthday cupcake, fed me pizza, and now we're in downtown Boston to celebrate with everybody else."

"Sorry I can't be there." The hurt was audible in Scott's tone.

"It's as if you were."

Only it wasn't. Not really.

There was a pause. Was Scott thinking the same? Instead, after a while, he asked, "Is David there?"

"He was." Haley didn't want to lie. "But he left early."

"Oh."

Was it an I'm-upset-he-was-there *oh,* an I'm-happy-he's-gone *oh,* or something between the two?

"Anyway," Haley continued. "I'm doing it more for the girls than for me. My birthday wish was to have an early night. I leave at five tomorrow morning."

"That's the saddest wish ever."

"Well, nothing great has happened lately."

"Haley?"

"Yeah?"

"Stare up at the sky."

Haley looked up at the dark blue sky. There wasn't a cloud in sight. "Okay?"

"Can you see the stars?"

"Uh-huh?"

"I'm looking at the same stars…"

Finally, a small smile crept on Haley's lips. "Are you going all cheesy romantic on me?"

"You bet I am! I promise you, Haley, this is the last birthday you spend alone."

"I wish I could kiss you right now."

"That sounds like a much better wish. Tilt your head up and send a kiss to the stars… They'll pass it over."

Feeling silly, but also giddily romantic, Haley gazed up, pressed her hand to her mouth, and blew a kiss to the sky. "Done! It should get to you in approximately… mmm… six hours, assuming kisses travel as fast as planes."

"I won't go to bed until it gets here. Now, go

enjoy your party. I love you."

"I love you, too."

With one last glance at the sky, and then at the spot where David's truck had disappeared, Haley walked back inside the bar.

***

The day after the birthday party, she left for Buffalo. Her mom had been super excited when Haley had announced she'd fly over to celebrate her birthday with them, and that she'd stay home for as long as she could. It had been ages since she'd stayed in Buffalo for more than a few days. Usually, even for the holidays, Haley never stayed more than a week.

At first, between the celebrations, the catching up with her parents, and the rest of the family's entourage—grandparents, aunts, uncles, cousins, and old friends—it was a family-reunion honeymoon. Haley was so grateful her dad was home that she didn't care about following the lifestyle of a fifty-five-year-old couple.

But after almost two weeks at home, Haley— as much as she loved her parents—couldn't stand living with them any longer. Her dad, usually the life of the party, was mostly sulky about his new healthy-but-unsavory diet. And her mom had started bugging Haley about all kinds of annoying house chores. The day Miranda Thomas told her she should clean up her room, Haley knew she had to get back to Boston. It was only ten days before the official year start, and every single one of her friends was going crazy over the massive end-of-summer party Blake Donovan was throwing.

Blake was on the basketball team, and was also apparently a rich kid with a summer house in the country, complete with an Olympic-size outdoor pool. And since his parents were away in Europe, he'd decided to put the empty house to good use.

In their roomies WhatsApp group, Madison wouldn't stop going on and on about the party—for a generally quiet introvert, she had a weird love for parties—but even Alice showed some excitement. Haley was torn; the date of the party would be only a day after Scott came back from California. She wasn't at all sure she'd be ready to share him with the world after only one night together.

But, party or not, Haley craved to be home in her own apartment. Free to eat or not eat at whatever weird hour of the day or night she pleased. Free to leave her dirty socks on the floor for as long as she liked without the socks police—aka her mom—yelling after her. And as much as she loved her dad, she was too young to follow his no-salt-no-bacon-no-nothing-remotely-yummy diet. Definitely time to hug her parents goodbye and go.

Twenty-five

Haley

Despite her flight being over an hour late, Haley was in a positive mood when she landed in Boston late on Friday night. Only a week until the party. And only a week before Scott came back from California. She took an Uber home and after a quick hello to her roommates, she went to bed.

But sleep didn't come easy; Haley was too excited. Scott was coming home in only seven days. How would it be to finally have him back?

Excitement quickly turned to worry. What if California had changed Scott?

And what if being alone here has changed me?

If nothing else, one thing had already changed for sure.

When Scott had left, Haley had positively hated his brother. But now they were friends of sorts, and David… he loved her, and she hadn't told Scott about his confession. Should she? Did Scott know anyway? No matter how much the two brothers claimed not to stand each other, they always seemed to get the other like no one else could.

Would it be weird to go to Scott's apartment

and see David there?

Yeah-ah.

David had promised not to be a jerk anymore, and that he wouldn't try to come between her and Scott. And Scott had seemed to accept Haley's friendship with his brother after her dad's heart attack. But would the three of them all living in the same city again tip the balance?

The next morning, Haley was still nervous. As always when she needed to calm down, she turned to coding. Only she didn't have an assignment or any inspiration for a new program. She just sat there staring at the black screen while fidgeting with the necklace David had given her for her birthday. Since that day, she'd never taken it off or used the USB key hidden inside. Haley weighed the ball of metal in her hand and then, on impulse, she opened the locket and plugged the tiny key into her laptop.

The memory was empty except for a folder called *Miss Robot*. Haley opened it. Inside there was a single JPEG file also named *Miss_Robot*. With trembling fingers, Haley clicked on the picture.

A black and white portrait popped up on the screen, its lines crude and sharp, but the final result no less powerful for it. Haley stared transfixed at the raw sketch of her face.

Was this how David saw her? Beautiful, but

strong and also… mysterious. It wasn't so much that she looked pretty in the drawing. It was the expression he'd immortalized—one of deep concentration Haley had never seen on herself—that struck Haley. Yeah, maybe she'd never seen that expression because when it came on she was too busy with whatever she was doing to look in a mirror.

And who would've guessed bad-boy David Williams had an artistic side? And was he really that much of a bad boy anyway? Or was it a mask he wore? A different kind from the one he'd had on the night they'd met. Was it a cover he put on every day to pretend nothing touched him when the exact opposite was true?

Haley still had David's number saved on her phone from the night Madison had forwarded her the contact for her to call him and ask if he'd told Scott about the kiss. She couldn't help but scoff and shake her head at the memory. That David had been a royal D-bag. But not the David who had driven seven hours to get her home to her sick dad. And not the David who had told her in the most romantic summer storm that he loved her. And not the David who had drawn this sketch.

Rolling her phone in her hands—left, right, left—Haley was itching to call him. Maybe a call was too much; a simple text would be better. She typed an easy-going:

Hey

Unoriginal, but safe. He probably wouldn't even see it or hit her back, and then it'd be fine. Unfortunately, three pulsing dots appeared on the screen almost immediately; David was composing a reply.

Hey?

Haley could almost picture the surprised-but-pleased frown on his face.

I'm impressed by your drawing skills

Easy with your perfect posing skills

I wasn't posing

No, I know

You're a natural

Some time passed with neither of them texting until a bubble appeared again on Haley's screen.

The library is not the same without you

You there?

Yep, you still in Buffalo?

For no reason, Haley's heart beat super-fast as she typed:

No, in Boston

Got back last night

Want to grab a beer later?

That sounded dangerously like a date. And as if reading her mind, David's next text came in pronto:

It's not a date

Still, Haley did not reply.

> Okay, Miss Robot

> Let's do it this way

> I'll be at the Plough and
> the Stars

> The Irish Pub down Mass
> Ave.

> At around 7

> If you feel like joining

> You know where to find
> me

Haley finally typed.

> I'm not coming

> I'll still be there

In case you change your
mind

I won't

Never say never

Gotta get back to work
now

See you later?

Haley did not reply this time. She locked the screen and shut the phone in a drawer as if it had suddenly become radioactive. Texting David had been a bad idea. An awful, stupid, wicked idea.

***

The tiny clock window on Haley's laptop kept teasing her. She tried to concentrate harder on the job she was doing—she'd settled for updating her coding cheat-sheet with everything she'd learned over the summer—but the task was dull enough to leave her mind free to roam. Plus the little, ever-changing numbers on the digital clock and their implied meaning kept distracting her.

The house was silent. For once, both Alice and Madison were out, and Haley was left alone to listen to the sound of silence. Or, more like the sound of a thousand imaginary clocks ticking away the seconds inside her head.

At 6:28, she wondered what David was doing, if he was getting ready to go out. She imagined him at his house smiling his crooked smile in front of the bathroom mirror.

And at 6:39, Haley pictured him putting on his black leather jacket and walking outside the apartment.

For the next fifteen minutes, Haley mapped in her head David's walking progress from his house, up on Cambridge Street, left onto Prospect, and finally right onto Massachusetts Avenue.

At 7:05, Haley figured David must be at the Plough and the Stars waiting for her. How long would he wait before he accepted she wasn't going?

By 7:09, Haley realized she was already monumentally late, and she had to go now if she wanted to reach the pub before David left. Surely he wouldn't wait more than half an hour. He wasn't that desperate.

On impulse, she got up from her chair, making it scrape on the floor. No time to get changed. Haley checked herself out in the mirror; her eyes were red from staring at a screen all afternoon, and her hair not as bouncy as if she'd just washed it. Her clothes were no better; her dark gray jeans and black flimsy tank top over a white T-shirt weren't exactly sexy-wear, but David never seemed to have a problem with how she looked or dressed.

David.

Haley sat on the bed, fidgeting with the locket hanging from her neck. Was she really going to meet him? Why not? Why make such a big deal out of it? It was only a beer with a friend. No, it wasn't. David didn't want to be her friend, and Haley… she didn't know what she wanted. What?! No, no. She knew. She wanted to be with Scott one hundred percent. Nothing else. *No one else.*

Pity her boyfriend had almost disappeared in the last few days. Scott had been even more sparse than usual with his texts and they hadn't talked in what seemed like forever. After two months without seeing him or talking to him for more than ten minutes at a time over the phone, Haley had started wondering—secretly, in a dark space at the back of her mind—if the epic romance she'd thought they'd shared had not entirely been inside her head. Scott would be home soon, true, but would their relationship be the same? Could they just pick up where they'd left as if nothing had changed?

And was seeing David an unasked-for

complication?

Oh, forget it. She could go have a beer with David without it having any apocalyptic, life-changing meaning. It was only a drink.

Right.

Haley stood up, grabbed her leather bag from the chair next to the desk, and walked down the hall of her apartment. Before opening the door, she fished out a tube of lip gloss and coated her lips in front of the hallway mirror, smacking them together in an imaginary kiss. There, she was ready.

Grabbing her keys from the plate on the small cabinet propped against the entrance wall, Haley threw the apartment door open and gasped, blinking several times while the rest of her body froze in utter shock.

Scott was standing on her doorstep. In the early sunset light filtering through the hallway windows, his perfectly tousled curls shone dark honey-gold, streaked with sandy highlights from his summer in California. His skin was tanned and dotted with even more adorable freckles than usual. His ripped chest and arms made Haley want to be crushed into a never-ending embrace. And his lips, curled up at the corners in a timid, nervous smile, were begging to be kissed.

Haley's pulse raced and butterflies exploded in her belly. How could she have thought even for a second not to be in love with Scott? Now that he was standing in front of her, it was clear her feelings hadn't changed. She'd never stopped loving him. Scott was her guy. It would always be Scott.

"Hey," Scott said.

Haley's lips broke into a wide, incredulous grin. "You're back a week early."

"Surprise."

"Is that why you disappeared in the last few days?"

A mischievous smile appeared on his face. "Are you mad?"

"No." Haley shook her head.

"Going somewhere?" Scott asked, tilting his chin toward the bag looped over her shoulder.

Haley blinked, confused. She honestly couldn't remember where she was headed. "No, I wasn't going anywhere," she said. She stared into Scott's sparkling green eyes a moment longer before he pulled her close and their lips collided.

To Be Continued

Note from the Author

Dear Reader,

I hope you enjoyed *My Best Friend's Boyfriend.* Thank you for sticking with the series so far. It means the world that you're still here with me.

Book four in the series, *I Don't Want To Be Friends,* will focus again on your favorite foursome: Madison, Haley, and the Williams brothers, and I hope you'll want to keep following them on their journey.

Which brother do you prefer? Bad-boy David or sweet-hottie Scott?

Now I have to ask you a huge favor. If you loved *My Best Friend's Boyfriend,* **please leave a review** on the retailer website where you purchased the book, or Goodreads, or wherever you like to post reviews (your blog, your Facebook wall, your bedroom wall, in a text to your best friend...) Reviews are the biggest gift you can give to an author, and word-of-mouth is the most powerful means of book discovery.

Thank you for your constant support!

Camilla, x

Acknowledgments

The first huge thank you goes to my readers. You make my work meaningful, enjoyable, and rewarding. Without your constant support, I wouldn't keep pushing through the blank pages.

Thank you to my editors Michelle Proulx and Helen Baggott for making my writing the best it could be.

And thank you to my family and friends for your constant encouragement.

Interior image credits: Freepik.com

www.ingramcontent.com/pod-product-compliance
Lightning Source LLC
Chambersburg PA
CBHW020138310726
48970CB00006B/1933